BABY SISTER

Also by Marilyn Sachs

MARILYN SACHS

BABY SISTER

E. P. DUTTON   NEW YORK

Library of Congress Cataloging in Publication Data

Sachs, Marilyn.
  Baby sister.

Summary: Fifteen-year-old Penny enjoys living in the
shadow of her idolized older sister, who is quirky,
self-centered, impossible, and loved by everyone.
  [1. Sisters—Fiction] I. Title.
PZ7.S1187Bab 1986 [Fic] 85-16171
ISBN 0-525-44213-8

Published in the United States by E. P. Dutton,
2 Park Avenue, New York, N.Y. 10016

Published simultaneously in Canada by
Fitzhenry & Whiteside Limited, Toronto

Editor: Ann Durell   Designer: Isabel Warren-Lynch

Printed in the U.S.A.   W   First Edition
10 9 8 7 6 5 4 3 2

with love to Anne Sachs

1

"No!" Cass was yelling. "No! No! No!"

"But I was only trying to find your bus pass," I told her.

She put her face up close to mine. Her breath made warm, wet spots on my cheek. "No, you weren't," she said. "You were snooping again. Weren't you?"

Yes, of course I'd been snooping. I always snooped when she wasn't around. I couldn't help myself. But that day I should have been safe. I had heard her leave. I heard the door slam behind her. Saturday morning—she was playing tennis at ten o'clock with Carol Kuhn. My parents were both downstairs, lolling over breakfast and reading the newspaper. I should have been safe.

I stood in the doorway and peered inside. The shutters on her windows were still closed, the bright daylight outside outlining each wooden slat. But inside, a soft darkness hovered. I loved her room, loved the way her things lay all over the place—on her bed, her chair and even on the floor. What a slob she was, I marveled. How Mom always had to keep picking up after her, screeching at her, threatening, ". . . the last time, Cass. After this, I'm just going to leave everything where it is. I'm going to take your friends in and show them what a slob you are. . . . The last time . . ."

I moved slowly into the room, savoring it. I had it all to myself. Why hurry? She should be gone at least two hours. Her bed was unmade—naturally. Cass never made her bed. She said it was a silly, archaic custom, and that she should be able to do whatever she liked in her own room. Mom screeched some more. "When you're on your own, you can live in a pigsty. But as long as you're in this house . . ."

Generally Mom made Cass's bed. Cass didn't want Mom to make her bed, but she didn't make a fuss if Mom came and went in her room when she wasn't there. She knew Mom wouldn't snoop. Mom didn't know where Cass hid her diary, and probably she didn't care.

Books and papers, pencils, records, letters all jumbled together. A pair of Adidas lay on their sides looking into each other's laces. A white half-slip with torn lace lay flung over her chair. I sat down on her bed and tried to make believe this was my room, that I was Cass. But I never could get away from myself because the first thing I always did in my mind was straighten everything up. Hang up the skirts and dresses. Pick up the dirty underwear. Make the bed. Clear off the desk. Throw out the papers. Sew up the torn lace. Turn Cass's wild, dirty room into a neat, dull room like my own.

No, I couldn't be Cass no matter how hard I tried.

I got off the bed and opened the blinds. As the sunlight entered, tiny specks of dust turned and twisted in the yellow light. Cass had flung her shimmery, black satin dress from the Salvation Army thrift shop on top of the desk. It upset me to see that it had knocked over the picture of herself and Gary at the junior prom. There was a big stain smack in the front of the dress, and I tried to figure out what it was. Cass and Gary had gone to a party the night before. I ran my fingers around the

2

stain's outline, wondering if it could be removed. I would have rushed the dress to the cleaners, but Cass never worried about how her clothes looked. If Mom didn't have it cleaned, she would just go on wearing the dress, and nobody would even notice. Maybe they would notice, but most likely they would be so busy looking at Cass herself that it wouldn't matter what she was wearing or how badly stained it was.

I restrained myself from hanging up the dress, but I did pick up the picture. I shouldn't have. Cass had forbidden me ever to go into her room when she wasn't there, so I had to be careful not to leave any traces. But I couldn't bear for the picture to lie there on its face. I picked it up and looked at them—Cass and Gary. Then I sat down on the chair, right on top of underwear, pajamas, books and a roll of Scotch tape—and I kept looking at the picture.

"How does she do it?" people always asked. Lots of other kids went to secondhand shops to buy clothes, but nobody looked the way Cass did in them. I had to laugh when I looked at that picture. I knew for a fact that all the other girls had worn new dresses to the prom. But not Cass. She was wearing a nightgown— one of those ordinary, sleazy, peach-colored nylon nightgowns—and on her head sat a big, floppy straw hat with flowers and ribbons. Under the nightgown she wore a black leotard and black tights, so you could see very clearly the outline of her body. Cass is no little skinny thing either, like me, so there was quite a bit to see.

In the picture she had her head down, and her big, green yellow cat's eyes shone out at you with that special Cass look—half laughter, half disdain. Cass's hair is the same color as her eyes—green yellow. She is the only one I know with hair that color. "An unwashed, disappointed blonde," Reba Harrison once said to Jackie Prentiss, who told Rich Armour, who told Gary. Cass laughed when she heard, and she washed her hair, but the color didn't change.

Gary's hair is really blond. Not a white blond but a bright golden yellow blond. Nobody has ever made fun of Gary's hair or any other part of him. He was always gorgeous, even back in fifth grade. According to Cass, that was when he started belonging to her, after he broke his thumb at the class picnic trying to tag her out in kickball.

Gary didn't look happy in the picture. He had wanted to wear a tux to the junior prom, but Cass made him wear a zoot suit from the forties. It had pegged pants, a long jacket and a key chain that fell down to his knees. And a big fat tie with big fat cats on it. He didn't look happy, but even in the zoot suit, he looked gorgeous.

I always thought Gary was wonderful, and I always felt proud and happy whenever he noticed me. Baby Sister, he used to call me, and sometimes he liked to try out new judo moves on me. I loved it when he picked me up and slung me around his shoulders. He never could do that with Cass because she is such a big, tall girl, even for a strong, powerful guy like Gary.

I used to giggle my head off, and Cass always stood there grinning. But once, when he dropped me, she screamed at him and said he was a clumsy jerk.

Cass screamed at him a lot. And sometimes she grew so angry, she wouldn't talk to him for weeks. Or see him. Sometimes she even went out with other guys. But he hardly ever got sore at her or went out with anybody else. He wrote her letters or left notes for her.

4

Dear Cass,

*I love you, Cass, you know that. Why do you do this
to me? I saw you with Ted Kurtzman today in the cafeteria. You knew I was there. You hung all over him to
make me jealous. Why do you do it, Cass? I told you I
was sorry. I don't even know for what. I can't even remember what it was all about. What do you want from
me, Cass?*

His notes. Jammed in her desk, on the floor, under
the bed, stuffed in books on her bookshelves— Why,
Cass, why?

Only one thing Cass cared about enough to hide. But
I knew where it was. I knew a lot about Cass she didn't
know I knew. In the second drawer on the left-hand
side of her desk, under her class pictures and history
report on Ulysses S. Grant. You had to reach back, all
the way back, because it was in a little book with pictures of unicorns on the cover. And inside, Cass wrote
in a tiny, tiny, very neat handwriting. Not every day.
Not even every week. Sometimes she skipped a few
months. I knew it all by heart, and I had favorite pages
that I read over and over again.

*They're jealous of me. "You think you're so superior
to all of us," Reba Harrison told me after English today. "You're always trying to show us up." Just because Ms. Berger read Reba's review of Camus' The
Stranger, and asked the class to comment. I didn't raise
my hand. Nobody did. I suppose because most of the kids
considered it a good piece of work. I thought it was driv-
el, and so I naturally didn't raise my hand. But Ms.
Berger called on me anyway. I tried not to attack its*

fundamental ignorance. I merely said it was "well meaning." So much for generosity. It's never appreciated.

All A's again. Rick Armour and Debra Gin act as if they don't have to work. As if the A's just settle on them effortlessly. As if they don't even care what kind of marks they get. Liars! They work, and they care. So do I, but I'm honest. I care a lot, and I work hard and I get A's. Competitive? Well, sure, I'm competitive. It wouldn't be much of a life if you didn't have to struggle against somebody else. But so far it's been easy. I worry about Penny. She just goes limp at the thought of hard work and struggle. I keep telling myself it's because she's young, but when I was her age . . .

Larry Foster trailing me again. Followed me out of the library and acted like he was surprised to see me. Walked me home and said how I was wasting my time with Gary. "He's a birdbrain," Larry said. "What can you talk to him about?"
"Who talks?" I told him.

Gary and me. Mm, mm, mm! "I'm never going to let you go," he said to me. Then he waited for me to say it back to him, but I didn't. He looked disappointed, but it didn't stop him from kissing me all over. And over. And over. He was making too much noise, so I told him to shut up. "What are you worried about?" he said. "Your parents are out visiting your Aunt Celia. There's only Baby Sister downstairs watching TV."
"No," I said. "She's only pretending to watch TV. She's listening to us. She's always listening. She has no life of her own."

6

"Oh, cut it out," Gary said. "She's a good kid. You pick on her too much. Leave her alone."

Leave her alone? If I left her alone, she'd grow up to be like Mom. I'm not going to let that happen.

She caught me holding the diary in my hands. All because Carol Kuhn forgot to show up at the tennis court. For the first time, she caught me with the evidence right in my hands. But at first she didn't see it.

"I was just looking for your bus pass," I said.

"No! No! No!" she yelled and leaped at me.

"Ma!" I screamed.

"STAY OUT OF MY ROOM!" she chanted, grabbing my shoulders and giving me a hard, furious shake to match each word.

"Ma!"

Finally, she pushed me down on her unmade bed, right on top of the rumpled sheets and blankets. Arched me over them and held me down by my shoulders. Her green yellow cat's eyes blazed at me with no laughter in them at all. "You're a sneak and a liar and a . . . a . . . ." That's when she suddenly saw the diary. ". . . a thief!"

I was still holding the diary in my hand, and she grabbed it away from me and began crying. Cass hardly ever cried. "You . . . you . . . you read my diary. . . . You . . . you . . . ."

"No," I whimpered. "No, Cass, honestly Cass. . . . "

Then she began tearing it—pulling out pages and ripping them up. My diary! It was mine as much as hers.

"Aaah!" I howled and flew at her, but she knocked me aside and kept ripping pages out of the book—tearing them and tearing them.

7

I tried to bite her arm, but she gave me another shove, and then Mom came running into the room.

"What's going on in here?" Mom yelled.

Cass kept right on tearing out the pages.

"Stop her!" I yelled. "She's tearing up the diary. Stop her!"

"Will you look at this place," Mom yelled. "My God! I just cleaned it up yesterday, and look at it. Your Aunt Celia and Uncle Henry are coming over, and just look at this room."

I flung myself at Cass and tried to tear the diary out of her hands, but she kicked at me and kept right on tearing page after page after page.

"Will you stop that this minute," Mom said. "Both of you. Stop!"

Then Cass stopped. She had torn up every page in her diary, so she stopped. She pointed her finger at me and said to Mom, "Get her out of here. I'm going to put a lock on my door and if she ever so much as comes in here—ever again—I swear to God, I'll kill her."

2

She never did put a lock on her door. And after a while, she started a new diary. It was an ordinary brown-covered one which she hid behind the mirror over her chest. It took me weeks to find it.

That was at the beginning of her senior year. I was just a sophomore. Gary came over all the time then.

"Doesn't he have a home of his own?" Mom grumbled when he wasn't around. But she liked Gary, and many times she let him stay for dinner.

Daddy didn't like Gary. "He's not for her," he kept telling Mom.

"Why not?" Mom demanded. She always asked, even though she knew what he was going to answer. "He's a very nice boy."

"Yes," Dad admitted. "He is a nice boy. But he's not for her."

"And I like his family too. His mother is a little stuck-up, but his father is very good-natured. Last week, at Safeway, he helped me carry my groceries and load up the car. I had such heavy bundles, it was more than I could handle myself, I can tell you that. But the girls are never around when I need them, and who else is going to help me?"

Dad didn't answer Mom's second question. He concentrated on her first. "He's a nice boy, and I have nothing against him personally. But she's a brilliant girl. She'll go far, if she doesn't tie herself down with somebody like him."

Mom sniffed. "You always make a big fuss over her. So she gets good marks—that's not all you need in life. A good man isn't so easy to come by, and Gary is the kind of boy who'll grow up to be just like his father. She won't have to carry heavy bundles by herself and work her fingers to the bone."

"He has no ambition," Dad said.

"You mean because he doesn't get A's in everything? A lot of good that will do her when she tries to turn those A's into dollar bills."

"You know," Dad said, "sometimes I think you hate her. Any other mother would be proud to have a daughter like Cass."

"Well," said Mom, "I'd be a lot prouder if she did her share of the work around this place and picked up after herself. All you ever think about is Cass. You do have another daughter too, remember? You have Penny, and Penny is a lot neater and better natured than Cass. Cass picks on her all the time, and you always take Cass's part."

I was sitting right there in the room, but neither of them seemed to notice me. The conversation was beginning to heat up.

"Penny is a good girl," Dad said. "And I don't always take Cass's part, but sometimes Penny does annoy Cass very much. I can't always blame Cass for losing her temper."

"You always take Cass's part."

"No, I don't. But Penny should stay out of Cass's room when Cass isn't there, and Penny should . . ."

"Penny should, Penny should." Mom mimicked

Dad's slow, solemn way of speaking. "And what about Cass? What should Cass do?"

"Cass should not tie herself down with that dumb boy," Dad yelled, rising, and then the two of them went at it as they usually did sooner or later.

"Your father doesn't like me," Gary said to me one afternoon. We were sitting in the kitchen, and Mom was upstairs vacuuming. Those days, I generally hurried home from school to be with Gary. Cass often went to the library to study when she wasn't involved with her extracurricular activities or playing tennis.

"It's not that he doesn't like you," I said carefully. "He just thinks Cass is too young to be serious about anybody."

Gary bent his blond head down over the Band-Aid on one of his thumbs and began picking at its edges. He didn't say anything. I could see the cowlick in the center of his head—a great big one that seemed to have grown bigger over the past year.

"Gary, I think you're going bald," I told him.

"No," he said, "I'm not." But he put his hand up and touched his cowlick. "Boy, you're a bundle of fun today, Baby Sister. Don't you have anything else to do besides give me strokes?"

"Mom likes you," I told him. "I think she'd be happy if you and Cass got married."

"Where is Cass, anyway?" Gary stood up and looked out of the window, even though the kitchen window faces the back. "She was supposed to be home by four."

"She said you should wait."

"I know. She told me that in school."

"Me too. She said if I saw you, I should tell you to wait."

11

"Well, it's four thirty now, and I've got lots of other things to do."

"Like what?"

Gary's face, full of tight, irritated lines, turned toward me. I imitated it, and he started laughing.

"Come on outside, Baby Sister. I'll teach you some new judo moves." Gary had a black belt in judo, although I could never figure out when he had time to go for lessons. He spent so much time hanging around Cass.

We went out on the deck and worked out until Mom yelled that I should get ready for dinner. She didn't invite Gary this time, although he stood there, looking at her until she turned away.

Cass was already sitting at the dining-room table as we came back into the house.

"When did you get back?" Gary asked.

"Oh—about an hour ago." She grinned at him and made a face at me.

"Why didn't you tell me you were back?"

"I wanted to finish working on my report."

"Oh! Gary! . . . How are you?" my father mumbled, coming into the room and sitting down. "Well—and what's for dinner tonight?" he asked my mother.

"I was waiting for you since four o'clock," Gary said. I could hear the anger in his voice.

"Meat loaf," Mom said.

Cass picked up her napkin and dropped it into her lap. "I'll call you later," she said. "Bye."

"Don't bother," he said. "I won't be home."

Cass raised her eyebrows and said, loud enough for him to hear if he was listening, "The worm turns."

Gary wasn't home that night, because Cass called him

a few times. His mother said he was out, but she didn't tell Cass where he went. She came into my room.

"What are you doing?" she asked.

"I'm writing to Grandma."

Cass made a face. "Why are you doing that?"

"To thank her for the money she gave me for back-to-school clothes."

"I never bother to send her thank-you notes," Cass said. "She knows I'm always happy to get money. She doesn't expect thank-you notes."

"Yes, she does," I told Cass. "I'm sure she's hurt that you never acknowledge her gifts. You should always send a thank-you note to anyone who gives you a gift— even if the person is your grandmother."

Cass shook her head at me. Then she looked around my room and wrinkled up her nose. "You're like a little old lady, Penny. It's unnatural for a girl your age to spend all her time writing thank-you notes to her grandmother and cleaning up her room."

"I don't spend all my time," I told her.

"No, that's true. Sometimes you go to funerals, and lots of times you spy on me."

"Not anymore, Cass," I yelled. "You always say that, but I don't spy on you. Not anymore."

She was restless. She began prowling around my room, a mean look on her face.

"Don't pick on me, Cass, just because Gary isn't home."

"See!" She stopped moving and looked at me. "You were listening to me telephoning."

"No," I lied. "I just guessed."

"Bull!"

"Well, I don't blame him," I said. "It was mean of

you not to tell him you were home. You take him too much for granted."

"But he was having fun with you." Cass sounded almost defensive. "I had to finish writing that English report while I was still going strong. I didn't know it would take so long."

"I think Gary is wonderful," I told her. "I hope you'll marry him."

Cass grinned. "You need a boyfriend," she said. "When I was your age, I'd been through lots of boyfriends."

"You always went back to Gary, though," I told her. "And you were always beautiful. I'm nothing. Nobody likes me. Especially boys."

"Beautiful?" Cass stepped in front of my mirror and looked at her reflection curiously. The shadowy light from my desk lamp rippled across her green yellow hair and cast mysterious shadows on her face.

"I'm nothing," I repeated.

Reluctantly, Cass tore her eyes away from the wonderful reflection in the mirror and looked at me in disgust. "Will you stop saying that!" she said angrily. "Stop listening to Mom, and stop writing those dumb thank-you notes."

"Nobody likes me," I continued. "I thought Frank Dean liked me once, but he only wanted me to invite him home because he had a crush on you."

"Listen, Penny," Cass said, "I have an idea. You like Gary, right?"

"You know I think he's great."

"Okay. Okay. But how about his brother, Darryl?"

"Darryl?"

"Sure. Darryl. He's your age. He might even be a little older. But I know he's a sophomore. And he's very

14

good-looking—a lot like Gary, even though he has red hair."

"First of all," I said, "Darryl isn't interested in me. He's got a million girls after him. And second of all, he doesn't look anything like Gary. And third of all, I don't like him."

"Why didn't I think of it before?" Cass said. "I'm going to get Gary make Darryl take you out."

"No," I yelled. "I hate Darryl. He's a jerk, and I hate him."

"We could double," Cass said. "Oh, it will be marvelous—the four of us going out together."

"I won't," I said.

"I'll fix you up and make you look like a sex goddess instead of a prune. You can even wear my tie-dyed red and blue blouse."

"It's dirty."

"How do you know it's dirty?"

"Your things are always dirty."

"Well, wash it, then. But it will look great with your blue eyes. And here, take that dumb thing off. You don't need it."

Cass pulled me out of my chair, spun me around, and put her hands up the back of my blouse, unfastening my bra.

"Cass!"

"You need to show off the little you've got," she said, laughing. Then she unbuttoned my blouse and yanked it off, along with the bra. She stood me there, naked to the waist, and walked around me, inspecting.

"Little, thin girls look sexy if they wear tight clothes and jiggle."

"I don't want to wear tight clothes and jiggle. Please, Cass, let me put on my shirt."

15

"No. Just a minute. You see, Penny, you're giving off all the wrong signals. You wear all those baggy, blah clothes, and you make yourself look run-of-the-mill. You have to let boys know that fires are burning inside you."

"No, they're not," I said, "and I'm getting cold."

She continued to circle.

"You don't want to be like Mom, do you?" she said.

"I want to be like you."

Cass said, "You can't ever be like somebody else. You have to find out what the real you is and let it all hang out. You have to take a few chances."

"Please, Cass, give me back my bra."

She threw it back to me but continued circling. "I'm going to fix you up, Penny. You're going to look wonderful."

"No, Cass, please. The last time you dressed me up— for Heidi's party—all the kids laughed at me and said I looked like a weirdo."

"Nobody will laugh at you this time," she promised.

16

3

"You're not going out like that?" Mom said.

"Cass said I look gorgeous," I told her.

Cass had taken me for a haircut the day before, and my hair rose up in spiky points all over my head. We had also stopped at the Salvation Army thrift shop, and she had made me buy a pair of faded purple striped jeans that were too tight.

"I can't sit down in them," I complained.

"So stand," Cass said.

Then she made me wear her red and blue tie-dyed shirt, which was way too large for me, and a belt made out of rope. I looked like a punker. Especially after she had plastered my face with makeup.

"You look like a freak," Mom said. "Go upstairs and get into some decent clothes. And wash your face!"

"Leave her alone," Cass yelled from her room. "She looks great. Like a model out of *Seventeen*."

"Like a model for a circus," Mom said. "Everybody will laugh at you, Penny. Go and change."

Cass came hurrying down the stairs. She was also wearing tight jeans—red ones—an oversized orange sweater and a wide leather belt. Her green yellow hair hung in wet curls all over her head, and her face—like mine—was plastered with makeup. But she looked wonderful. Whatever Cass did, she always looked wonderful.

"Just leave her alone," she said to Mom. "It's time she looked like a normal teenager instead of a dried-up old lady."

"She looks stupid," Mom yelled. "She looks like a clown. Do you want everybody to laugh at her?"

Dad cleared his throat. "Linda," he said to Mom, "maybe this is the style. Maybe we're just not up on the latest fashion for girls."

"Just look at her," Mom screeched, waving her hand at me. "Don't tell me about fashions. Just look at her."

"Well . . ." Dad said, "well . . ."

"We have to go now." Cass grabbed my arm. "We've got to go get Penny a man."

"She'll never get a man looking like that," Mom said.

Of course she was right. I didn't get a man, but probably it wouldn't have made any difference what I looked like.

"So what do you want to do?" Darryl asked me.

It was one of those mild late September evenings, and we were down at Ocean Beach. Gary and Cass were chasing each other around down at the water's edge.

"I don't know," I said. "What do you want to do?"

He laughed—a stupid, coarse laugh—and I said quickly, "We could take a walk."

"Not safe," Darryl said. "Too many junkies around on this beach."

Then he told me about how he and "a friend" (he didn't say whether it was a girlfriend or a boyfriend so I guessed girl) had been mugged on the beach not far from here only a week or so ago by a gang of "pot heads." "And during the day too. This place is even worse at night. I don't know why Gary wanted to come here."

"It was Cass's idea."

"He does everything she wants," Darryl said. "It's disgusting."

"I don't think it's disgusting. They're in love."

"He's a jerk," Darryl said. "He doesn't have any self-respect. She walks all over him, and he lets her."

"She doesn't walk all over him."

"She's a bitch," he said. "I hate her."

"Don't talk about my sister like that," I yelled. "What do you know about her? What do you know about anything?"

"I know she's made him into a dishrag. He's not himself around her. My parents hate her too. Nobody in my family likes her."

"So why did you come tonight?"

"Because I was curious." Darryl looked at me and shook his head. "I wasn't even sure who you were. Gary said you were like Cass, and I was curious, but . . ."

"I'm not like her," I said, "but I wish I were."

"No," he agreed, "you're not like her." His eyes moved over me as if I were a sack of potatoes. "You're nothing like her, but don't wish you were."

"I'm nothing," I said, "but she's . . ."

"She's a bitch," Darryl said, "and you're lucky you're not like her. It's better to be nothing than to be a bitch. At least you don't hurt anybody. You don't make anybody do dumb things and make them feel like dirt."

Cass was riding piggyback on Gary's shoulders. We could hear her laughing from down by the water's edge.

"Everybody hurts somebody," I said, and then I stopped, surprised, not really sure what I meant.

"What's that supposed to mean?"

"I don't know."

"Are you trying to point a finger at me because of Barbara Cummings?"

"Who's Barbara Cummings?" I said.

"Oh, come on. You must have heard some stories about her and me. She's been blabbing all over school."

"I don't know who you're talking about, but, see—somebody always gets hurt in a relationship."

"What kind of relationship?" Darryl said angrily. "I went around with her a few months, and she began acting like she owned me. The last thing I want is to get stuck with one girl, like Gary. His life isn't his own."

"He's lucky," I cried. "Cass is so smart and so beautiful and so—well—so different from any other girl. There's only one Cass in the whole world."

"Thank God!"

"And she loves Gary. I know she does. Most of the time, I mean."

"Most of the time," he murmured. "No guy wants that most of the time stuff. He wants a girl to want him all the time."

"Like you?" I cried. "You don't want anybody all the time."

"See," Darryl said. "I knew Barbara told you."

"I don't even know Barbara. But you don't want to settle with just one girl. Why should Cass settle with one guy? I mean—one of these days I know she will. But right now she's just not ready."

"It's different for girls," Darryl said slowly.

"No, it isn't."

"What do you know? I bet you never go out at all."

"Well . . ." I said, "well . . ."

"It's okay, Penny. A girl doesn't have to make the rounds. Listen to me. It's not good for girls to make

20

the rounds. And whatever they say, guys respect girls who are not easy." He put a hand on my arm and gave it a pat. I shook it off angrily.

"You sound like you belong in the nineteenth century," I told him.

He shrugged. "Well, it's the truth. Nineteenth, twentieth, twenty-first. I bet nothing will change. A guy likes to be the one who asks, and he likes a girl who—well—kind of resists a little bit—at first."

"You mean a girl who plays games? A girl who acts a part because some dumb guy thinks she should act that way? This is the twentieth century, Darryl. Women aren't men's playthings anymore. Haven't you heard?"

I was breathing hard, and, suddenly, I began feeling like I was somebody else. Like I was Cass. I didn't usually go around saying things like that.

But Darryl wasn't listening to me. He was watching Gary and Cass lying down together on the sand, their arms around each other.

"The bitch!" he said.

"Well?" Cass asked me later that night. "Did you have a good time?"

"No," I said.

"Why not? It seemed to me the two of you had plenty to say to each other. Every time I looked at you, you were deep in conversation."

"You didn't look very hard," I said. "You and Gary were too busy making out to notice. But I wasn't deep in conversation with Darryl. Most of the time we didn't have anything to say to each other at all. And when we did talk, we argued. He's a jerk, and he hates you."

"No, he doesn't."

"Yes, he does. He called you a bitch, and he told me he hates you. He said his parents hate you too. They all think you make a dishrag out of Gary."

"Little Darryl said that?" Cass laughed. She was stretched out on her bed, and I was sitting on the edge. I was happy to be there with her, even though the evening had been such a bust.

"Yes, he did," I said. "But who cares what he says?"

"I do," Cass said. "I care what everybody says. Don't you?"

"No. I don't care what people say. Not if I don't like or respect them. I only care if they're people who matter to me."

"I care," Cass said. She was lying on her bed, her hair rippling all over her pillow. Her face looked flushed and serious.

"You don't act like you care. Lots of people don't like you. Lots of people are jealous of you, but you don't care about them. You always do exactly what you want."

"I do care," Cass insisted. "I can't help myself, but I care."

"And you don't care what Gary thinks. You're always making Gary feel bad."

"No, I'm not," she said. "I love Gary. I want Gary to be happy."

"You do love Gary?" It made me feel very happy to hear her say it. "Are you going to marry him?"

"Are you kidding, Penny? I'm seventeen years old. I'm not going to get married for a long, long time. I've got a lot to do first."

"Gary will wait for you. If you tell him, he'll wait."

"I know. I can do anything I like with Gary."

"So tell him to wait."

"No!" Cass stayed quiet for a moment, thinking. Then she said, "He's really not for me, Penny."

"That's what Daddy says. He thinks he's not good enough for you. He thinks if you tie yourself down with Gary, you won't accomplish anything."

"Daddy is wrong," Cass said. "If Gary and I hook up, it will be bad for Gary. It won't make any difference for me. Nothing's going to stop me."

"You'll make him happy," I said. "Tell him to wait."

"I don't know." Cass shook her head on the pillow. "If I really wanted him to be happy, I'd let him go. He's not for me. And I'm bad for him. I make him miserable. But I can't let him go. Not yet."

I couldn't stand thinking about Cass letting Gary go, and I started crying.

"What are you blubbering about?"

"I don't want you to let him go. I want you to marry him and make him happy."

Cass stood up and put her arms around me. "You really are like a little old lady," she murmured. But she rocked me in her arms until I stopped sniffling. Then she pushed me away and looked at me.

"You're the one we have to talk about, Penny. We've got a lot of talking to do about you."

"I don't want to talk about me. There's nothing to talk about."

"Stop it!" she said. "There's lots to talk about. What you want to do with your life . . ."

"I don't know," I told her. "I just want to be happy. I keep telling you that."

"You've got to make some plans. You're a sophomore now, and next year you take the P.S.A.T.'s. You

23

have to get high scores so lots of colleges will be interested in you. You need to improve your grades too, so you can pick and choose when the time comes."

"I'm not going to college. I keep telling you."

"Yes, you are! You are going to college, and you are going to a good one far away from home. You are going to spread your little wings and learn all about the big world out there."

"I want to stay home. I don't care about the big world out there."

"I can't believe you," Cass said.

"I keep telling you."

"You're a late bloomer," Cass said. "Some girls don't really get started until late in their teens. You're just young for your age. You don't have to decide now."

"I'm fifteen," I told her. "I don't like school. I never liked school, and I don't like to study. I'm not going to college. I'll get a job when I graduate. Maybe one day, I'll get married. . . ."

"And end up like Mom?" Cass smirked.

"What's wrong with Mom?"

"Everything. She spends the whole day wrapped around housework. She whines all the time, and she doesn't know or care about anything that goes on outside her house. You could drop a nuclear bomb outside her kitchen window, and she wouldn't notice."

"She's happy," I said. "She just complains a lot."

"She fights with Daddy all the time, and he's hardly ever home."

"He has all those patients." (My father is a psychologist.)

"Oh, sure!"

"You mean—you think Daddy is having an affair?"

"An affair? Our father?" Cass burst out laughing. "I

24

wouldn't blame him if he was. All he gets from Mom when he's home is an earful of complaints. She's boring."

"You always take his part."

"No, I don't. He doesn't lift a finger around here, but it's really her fault. She likes it that way. She enjoys being a martyr. You don't want to end up that way, Penny. You have to be independent."

"I don't know," I said.

"I'm going to help you, Penny," Cass said. "I'm going to spend more time with you. We'll go to museums and concerts. You used to play the piano. How come you don't play the piano anymore?"

"I don't like to practice."

"And you have a nice voice. You should be in the chorus. How come you're not in the chorus?"

I shrugged my shoulders.

"Well, next term, I want you to sing in the chorus. And in the meantime, I think you should learn the guitar. Gary has one he never uses. He can lend it to you."

"I don't want to learn the guitar."

"You're going to learn the guitar. It will give you confidence. When you go to parties, it will make you the center of attention."

"Hardly anybody ever invites me to parties."

"And you should read more. Tomorrow, we'll go over to the library and take some books out for you."

"My eyes hurt when I read."

"Maybe from all the TV you watch. From now on, you're going to watch less TV and read more. I'm going to keep tabs on you from now on. I'm going to take better care of you."

I leaned my head against Cass's shoulder and half listened to all her plans for my development. How I loved her! It made me proud and happy that Cass, wonderful Cass, cared enough about me to spend time trying to make me into something I knew I could never be.

4

The next morning, she stopped me as I was leaving the house.

"Where are you going?" She came down the stairs, grabbed my shoulder and spun me around. "And why are you dressed like that?"

I was wearing my gray suit, a white blouse, pearls and black pumps. I had brushed down the spiky points in my hair and scrubbed all the makeup off my face.

"It's Catherine's Aunt Laura. You know—the nice one who took Catherine and me to the movies."

"No, I don't know. But where are you going?"

"Well, she died the day before yesterday, and today's the funeral."

"You're going to your friend's aunt's funeral?"

"Well . . . I thought I should. . . . I . . . ."

"Penny, you've got to stop going to funerals."

"This is only my third," I protested. "I only went to Warren Singer's father's funeral, and last summer, when Mrs. Carpenter's husband—you remember Mrs. Carpenter, Cass. She used to work in the stationery store on Geary, and she always gave me a special price on ball-point pens."

"I can't figure you out at all," Cass said. "You must be some kind of ghoul, going to all those funerals of people you don't even know or care about. I've never been to a funeral in my life. What is it with you?"

I hung my head. I hated it when Cass didn't approve of me. Mom came out of the kitchen, and Cass said, "Do you know she's going to a funeral again?"

"Yes," said Mom. "I told her not to go. I don't think a girl her age has to go to funerals."

"That's not the point," said Cass. "She wants to go."

Mom nodded at me. "Penny's very kind that way. She wants to pay her respects to Catherine's family. I don't think it's necessary, but she thinks they would appreciate her going."

"Bull," said Cass. "There's something about funerals that turns her on."

"How can you say such a thing?" I yelled. "I'm only doing what's right."

"Okay, Penny. Just go upstairs and get out of those dumb clothes. Today I'm devoting to you. Today, we're going to start turning you into a human being, so we'll need an early start. Let's go."

"No!"

"Yes!"

"Ma!"

Mom said, "Cass, you stop picking on Penny. She's old enough to know her own mind. And she looks a lot more human today than she did last night."

"I'm going," I said, hurrying out the door and avoiding Cass's eyes.

Catherine and her family were already inside the church, but she hadn't saved me a place as she had promised. I had to sit all the way at the back, because the church was filled with people. Catherine's aunt must have had a lot of friends, well-dressed ones too. I always enjoyed looking at the way people dressed at funerals. You hardly ever had the chance to see a whole bunch of people so fashionably dressed.

Of course weddings were better, but I didn't often get invited to a wedding. And you certainly could not go to a wedding without an invitation the way you could to a funeral. But how could I explain this to Cass? I settled back in my seat and looked around me.

I noticed a woman, sitting next to a man who looked a little like Burt Reynolds, wearing a beautiful blue outfit with a matching hat. Another woman, who came down the aisle by herself, was wearing a deep red dress with a wine-colored jacket and black shoes and gloves. Uh-uh, I thought. The wine is just a couple of shades off. It doesn't work. I hardly glanced at the two women who followed her in. Both were dumpy and wore poorly fitting nondescript suits. But behind them came a tall, slim, gorgeous woman in a peach-colored wool dress and a sleeveless tweed coat. Very, very nice.

Down front, an old lady was crying. You couldn't hear her, but an old man was patting her on the back, and a younger man was whispering something into her ear. The old lady must be Catherine's grandmother. She was wearing a very ordinary-looking brown coat.

I wondered what would happen if I died. It must be terrible for a mother if a child died first, even a middle-aged child like Catherine's aunt. My mother would cry, I knew that, and so would my father, even though he did like Cass better. And Cass? Would she cry? No—Cass wouldn't cry. Cass would come running down the aisle in the midst of all the whispering, fashionably dressed people. She would wear tight jeans and an oversized orange sweater, and her green yellow hair would whirl around her head in wet curls. She would

29

tear open the coffin where I lay dressed all in white with a wreath of pale pink roses on my head. She would pull me out and breathe life into me. She would never let me die.

But if Cass died? Gary would cry, and so would Mom and Dad. But what would I do? I would cry and scream, but I would never be able to bring her back to life. No! No! No! I hated to think of Cass dying. Because if she did, nobody would be able to make her live again.

The tears were rolling down my face. Up front, the organ had stopped, and the priest was speaking. Other people were crying too. Next to me, an old lady, wearing a black hat with frayed gray ribbons, began to dab at her eyes with a handkerchief.

I wasn't able to get a ride out to the cemetery, so I returned home after the service. Cass was waiting for me.

She made me change my clothes, and then we went off to the library.

"Here," she said, dropping book after book into my arms. "I want you to read this one, and this one and this one."

"But Cass—I can't read fast. You can only keep them for three weeks. Just pick out one."

"You can renew them. You have to read Kafka and Camus and Flannery O'Connor."

"I don't like foreign writers."

"Flannery O'Connor is American. She came from the South and wrote the most amazing stories. Unfortunately, she died young. . . ."

"What did she die of?"

"Leukemia, I think."

"Well, maybe I'll read her."

"Camus died young too," Cass said, "in a car crash.

If that's what it takes to get you to read, we shouldn't have any trouble at all. Lots of writers died young—Keats and Shelley and Emily Brontë. Hey—she would be a good one for you. How about *Wuthering Heights*?"

"I saw the movie."

"Oh, but this isn't anything like the movie. The lovers are savage and hateful. Oh—and Heathcliff—that's the man—he even digs up Cathy—that's the woman—after she's been dead for years and looks at her corpse. You should love that one."

"Don't make fun of me, Cass. You always make fun of me."

But I took *Wuthering Heights* out of the library, along with the other books. It was the only one I read. I didn't like it, but I read it anyway to please Cass.

Cass kept at me all the rest of that weekend. It was just after midterms, so she had a little time. Generally, she went on her binges of rehabilitating me between terms, after midterms and here and there during the summer.

She made Gary bring over his old guitar. Actually, it belonged to Darryl, but he said Darryl wasn't interested in it anymore. He didn't need it to be noticed at parties. Cass lined up a guitar teacher for me, and I had my first lesson that Sunday. I didn't want to go, but she made me. And she made Mom pay for the lessons.

"It's a waste of time," Mom said. "She took piano lessons for two years, and she never practiced unless I stood over her."

"I'll make her this time," Cass said.

"What's the point? She's old enough to know her own mind. If she's not interested, why bother?"

All of this was going on in the kitchen, with me sitting right there at the table while the two of them discussed me. In my family, nobody minded if I was around while they talked about me behind my back.

"Because she's got nothing inside her head right now except cleaning her room and going to funerals. It's not natural for a girl her age not to have any interests. When I was her age, I was already active in the antinuke movement. I was also on the tennis team, in the model UN and active in student government. Besides going out like crazy."

"I didn't like that," Mom said. "You know I didn't like the way you always stayed out late. I still don't like it."

"And I got A's in everything."

"You never had time to clean your room," Mom said.

"Penny has time to clean her room. But she doesn't do anything else. Is that what you want?"

"Penny's a good girl," Mom said. "I don't have to worry about Penny. She doesn't stay out late the way you do. She's a good girl, and if she doesn't have a lot of interests, that's the way she is. I was the same way when I was her age."

"That's just what I'm afraid of."

"Oh? And exactly what does that mean?"

"Oh, come on, Mom. You know what I mean."

"No, I don't," Mom said stiffly.

"Okay. Let's put it this way. Would you want Penny to end up the same way you did?"

"What's wrong with the way I ended up?"

"Lots of things," Cass said. "To begin with, you're not very happy."

"Who says I'm not happy?"

"You do, Mom. Every day you complain and you yell and you say Dad leaves you alone too much. You say you work too hard and that nobody appreciates you. Every day you say it, Mom."

"Well," said my mother, "that's life. It's not a bowl of cherries. But I'm married, I have children, I have a home. It could be a lot worse."

"It could be better too. Come on, Mom. Aren't you ever sorry you didn't do something else with your life?"

"No," said Mom, "I never am."

"Come on, Mom. You know you are."

"No."

"Mom?"

"Well . . ." Mom laughed suddenly, and so did Cass. I laughed too, but nobody noticed.

"You can't fool me," said Cass, waggling her finger at Mom.

"Cut it out, Cass," Mom said, giggling like a young girl. Her cheeks grew very pink, and her pale blue eyes shone.

"Okay. Just sit there, Mom."

Cass went flying off. You could hear her footsteps racing up the stairs.

"Your sister!" Mom said, turning to me. Noticing I was there. Dad always said how Mom favored me. It wasn't true, and I knew it. She adored Cass just as much as Dad and I did. Maybe even more. "You never know what she'll do next."

Cass's steps on the stairs, descending. She came into the room, grinning at Mom and holding the large picture Mom kept in her box of photographs. She laid it down in front of Mom, and Mom shook her head over it and sighed. In the picture, Mom—fourteen years old, small, skinny, looking a lot like me—stood smiling out of that old photo. She was wearing a blue and silver short ice-skating costume and white ice skates.

"Was that before or after you won the city competition?"

"After," Mom said.

"How good were you, Mom?"

"Oh!" Mom flung up her head. "I was good."

"As good as Dorothy Hamill?"

"Well, I don't know. We did different things then."

"Grandma said you were good," Cass insisted. "Grandma said you were good enough to get into the Olympics."

"Oh, your grandmother!" Mom laughed. Her cheeks were still pink, and she touched the old photo with one finger, smoothing it. "She's a lot like you, Cass. A real driver."

"She said you would have made the Olympic team if you hadn't met Dad."

"No, no," Mom said.

"She said she told you to take Spanish in high school, but you insisted on taking French. That's where you met Daddy, and after that your skating was never the same."

"No," Mom said. "It was just—Cass, you won't like to hear this—but I just lost it."

"What? You mean you met Daddy and you lost your interest in skating? I guess in those days it was either-or. You either had a love life, or you had a career. Thank God, Penny and I live now."

"No, no, you want me to say it like that. But that's not what it was. I lost it—my need to struggle, to compete. I didn't want to do it anymore. I didn't have the killer instinct, I guess, and all I wanted was to have fun."

"Like me," I said. "That's what I want—to have fun."

"But Mom," Cass insisted, "you had fun when you were skating, didn't you? Weren't you happy when you were performing all those great leaps and spins? Weren't you happy when you won all those prizes and everybody said you were the best?"

"Maybe," Mom said. "I don't remember."

"Grandma said you married Dad just to spite her."

"I married Dad," said my mother grimly, "because I loved him."

"But you could have gone on skating," Cass said. "Why did you give up skating?"

"Because I was finished with it." Mom pushed the picture away. "So, no, I don't have any regrets about that. You want me to say I do, Cass. You're like your grandmother that way. But you can't bully people into living the kind of life you think they should live. Penny will find her own way just as I did. I'm never sorry— never for one moment—that I gave up skating. I never regret that."

"So what do you regret?" Cass stood up, watching her.

Mom shook her head. "Nothing."

"Yes, there's something. I know there's something."

"There's nothing," Mom repeated uneasily. "Nothing really, except . . ."

"Except?" Cass cried triumphantly. "What, except?"

"Except," Mom said slowly, "maybe I was too young when I married. Maybe I should have waited. I mean, not that I didn't love your father, or that I don't love you two girls. But maybe I should have waited a little. Taken a job for a while. Had a little more fun."

You could see Cass was disappointed. I knew she wanted Mom to say she was sorry she hadn't become a champion skater or a champion something. But Mom was just sorry she hadn't had more fun. Mom could see that Cass was disappointed, so she said quickly and kind of angrily, ". . . and if Penny doesn't practice her guitar, I'm not going to pay for lessons. I'm not going to throw good money out just because you think she should learn. I'll give her one month and that's all."

5

Mom actually gave me three months, and by then it was clear to everybody that the guitar would not make any kind of change for the better in my life. Cass dragged me to a few parties with her and Gary, and once I even got invited to one on my own. On each occasion, I took the guitar with me. But even when Cass was there, insisting that I perform, nobody ever wanted to listen.

By Christmas, she had other things to think about, and I had finally found what I wanted to do with my life. It was a very happy time for me. I told Cass.

"Sew?" she said like she was going to throw up. "You want to sew?"

I felt giddy and light-headed, but I tried to tell her how it had happened to me. How the wonderful revelation had suddenly exploded inside me.

"It happened at Britex. You know, Cass, that big fabric store downtown."

"No," said Cass. "I don't know."

"Catherine asked me to go downtown with her to the Emporium. She wanted to get a pair of brown pumps to go with her brown velveteen skirt."

"Ugh!" said Cass.

"But Catherine's foot is very wide—a D width, and they didn't have her size at the Emporium."

"If Catherine would lose some weight, she wouldn't

look like such a blimp and her foot would be nar-rower," Cass said. She had never thought much of Catherine, who had been my best friend since third grade.

"Anyway," I continued, "we went to Macy's and I. Magnin's, and then we started looking at all the shoe stores on Geary—the Red Cross store is there and the Naturalizer."

"All the stores for fat, middle-aged women. Penny, what is the matter with you?"

"So we passed Britex and went into the shoe store, and as I was sitting there, as Catherine was waiting for the salesman, I remembered how the Britex store looked—the windows I mean—filled with stacks of materials in greens and reds and blues. Right then and there, in the Naturalizer store, it happened to me. Oh, Cass, I'm so happy!"

"I don't understand. What happened?"

"I don't know myself. I just said to Catherine, 'I'll be in the Britex store. Come and find me when you're finished.' Then I got up and ran back down the street and went into the store. It's a wonderful store—a great, big one. They have wools and silks and materials I never heard of all up and down the walls and on counters everywhere. I felt like crying because I was so happy. It felt like I had been lost and suddenly I found my way home."

"Penny, I'm beginning to think you're nuts."

"So when Catherine came to get me, she wanted to go home. They had the shoes she wanted in the Nat-uralizer store, so she said, 'Let's go home.' I told her I wanted to stay. I said she should go home. She said we could stop for some dessert first in Mama's, but I said no. I just wanted to stay in Britex. She got kind of sore, but she left. Cass, I stayed there for a couple of hours. I walked up and down, touching the materials. I went up to all the floors, even to the top. I looked at the trimmings and the buttons and even the elastic tapes. I kept breathing in all the good smells of new fabrics, and then I started looking through the pattern books. They're so beautiful, Cass, those books with the beautiful women wearing the most beautiful clothes. And they look so happy—the way I want to look."

"Will you stop talking like a wimp," Cass said between her teeth.

"I was the last one to leave. They practically had to throw me out. But now I know what I want to do. What I think I always wanted to do, but I didn't know it before. I want to make clothes."

"You mean," Cass said, beginning to look slightly more cheerful, "you want to be a fashion designer. It's a very competitive field, Penny, and considering that you've never shown much talent for drawing, I'm amazed, but . . ."

"I've always loved clothes," I said, bursting in. "I've always loved to look at well-dressed women. That's why I like funerals so much, but I never understood why until I passed that Britex window. Oh, Cass, I'm so happy!"

"Well," Cass said, "I suppose you could go to art school and learn fashion design. Personally, I find clothes kind of boring, but it could be an interesting career, I guess, fashion design."

"No, no," I said, "not fashion design. I'm not interested in that. I just want to sew."

"Sew what?"

"Anything. From patterns. From those beautiful patterns I told you about. I have to learn first. Just think,

I've never even sewn on a sewing machine before, but I know I'll love it. I guess I'll start with something easy like a wraparound skirt. And then I can try a dress, and maybe in a few months, Cass, I can start making clothes for the two of us."

Cass said, disgusted, "Penny, I think you're a throwback. You live in a world that's wide open for women. You could be anything you want—even president of the United States. But all you want to do is sew."

"I'm sorry, Cass," I said, bursting into tears. "I know you're disappointed in me, but you did say that one day I'd find out what I wanted to do, and that when I did, I should do it. Cass, I want to sew. That's what I want to do."

"Okay," Cass said with a nauseated look on her face, "go ahead and sew. I guess it's harmless, and maybe you are a late bloomer and we'll just have to wait until your real interest develops."

I asked my parents to give me a sewing machine for Christmas. They gave me one of those little portable ones without any fancy attachments, but I was happy. Cass and Gary went off skiing in Tahoe, and I stayed in almost all of Christmas week, sewing. I made myself a demin wrap skirt that came out perfect. I made two checked aprons for my mother, a flowered tablecloth and six matching napkins for my grandmother, a pink sundress for myself and finally a gathered skirt in a brilliant red and purple heavy cotton for Cass. I laid it on her bed, as an offering, before she came home from Tahoe.

It was the happiest week of my life.

Catherine invited me to go to the movies with her twice, and I turned her down. My parents asked me to go out to dinner with them once, and I refused. I don't remember what I ate or drank that week, but I was happy.

I only looked at Cass's diary twice.

He doesn't let me breathe. If I let him, he would spend all his time worshiping me. Love gets boring when it goes on and on. Everything and everyone gets boring. We all need breaks from loving. Even Romeo and Juliet would have gotten bored with each other if they had lived. How can he love me so much that nothing else is important in his life? It's frightening.

Penny's going to sew! That's all she wants to do with her life. Why should it matter so much to me? Because she's my sister? Because everything she does reflects on me? Because I love her and want her to be productive as well as happy? I hope that's the main reason. Why should she infuriate me so much? When I think of her—her neat little room, her neat little figure, her neat drawers and closets—I feel like choking. She's so young and all tidied up already. My own loose ends keep flapping in the wind. I hope I'll never be neat.

When Cass returned from Tahoe, I was working on a dress for myself in a wonderful shade of bright green. I heard her running up the stairs to her room, and I stopped sewing to listen. By now, she should have spotted the skirt stretched out on her bed. I smiled, thinking of her surprise when she discovered how accomplished I had become. Maybe she was picking it up now, holding it in front of herself as she stood before her mirror. Red and purple—two colors she loved. She had several red shirts and a couple of purple sweaters.

Mom had washed all her things while she was away. Maybe she was trying on one of the shirts with the new skirt.

Cass came storming into my room, holding the skirt away from her, between her thumb and forefinger.

"What is this?" she demanded.

"I made it for you, Cass."

"It's ugly." She tossed it on my bed and looked at me as if I had done something obscene. "Have you been up here all week, working on that thing?"

"Listen, Cass," I told her, "I've learned so much this week. I made myself a skirt and a sundress, and I made Mom two aprons, and a tablecloth and napkins for Grandma and the skirt for you. Now I'm really trying something hard. It's a fitted dress with a shirred bodice, set-in sleeves and a straight skirt."

"You spent all of Christmas week sewing?"

"Well," I said, "not all."

"You're fifteen years old," Cass said, "and you've spent a whole week making ugly things."

"No," I yelled, "they're not ugly. They're beautiful. Mom loves her aprons and Grandma . . ."

"Well, I hate this skirt. It's the ugliest thing I ever saw."

"I thought you would love it," I cried, the tears rolling down my cheeks. "It's almost exactly like the material on the pattern, and the girl looked just like you, except her hair was brown."

"I don't care if her hair was purple. Stop comparing me to somebody on a pattern, and stop making me ugly things."

"I was going to make you and Gary matching shirts," I wept.

"No!" Cass yelled. "Don't make me anything. Do you hear? I don't want anything from you. Get off my back."

Later, Mom told me Cass and Gary had broken up. "She's upset," Mom said. "So don't mind what she said about your sewing."

"She hated it. She thought it was ugly."

"No, no. She was just upset."

"But she's broken up lots of times with Gary. Why should she be upset?"

"She's says it's final this time."

I went downstairs to watch *Dallas*, my favorite program. When it was over, I came back upstairs and stood outside Cass's door.

"Go away," she said.

"Can I come in?"

"No."

I stayed outside, and Cass yelled, "You're breathing so loud I can't hear myself think."

"Can I come in?"

She didn't answer, so I opened the door and slowly walked into her room. Her skis, ski boots and jacket lay on the floor. She hadn't unpacked all her things, and some of them were still oozing out of her pack. The room was already a mess, even though Cass had been home only a short time.

"What do you want?" she said.

"I don't know." I gave her a weak, little grin. "I just wanted to say hello."

"Hello. Now go away."

"What's the matter, Cass? Why are you so angry?"

"I'm not angry."

"Yes, you are."

"Okay, I'll tell you why I'm angry. I'm angry because I have to come home to this stupid house and look at your stupid face and find that ugly, stupid skirt on my bed. I can't wait to get away. I can't wait."

"Well," I told her, "you'll be graduating in June and going away to school in September. It will be terrible for me and for Gary, but I guess you'll be happy to go."

"It will be the best thing in the world for Gary when I leave," she said. "Maybe he can start living then."

"What do you mean?" I sat down carefully on the bed, next to her.

"He can't breathe when I'm around," she said. "He can't enjoy himself, can't think, can't let me live. He's a great skier, but he hung around me the whole week. He never went off, not once, by himself. I told him to, but he was always there, behind me, in front of me, on one side of me. Once—only once—I thought he'd gone off by himself. I was skiing with a couple of other kids on one of the steeper ridges. It was a little hard for me, but I was managing. There was a patch of ice coming up—I saw it, and I was going to move around it. Suddenly I heard somebody yelling, and I turned. It was Gary, trying to warn me. I could have been killed, but somehow I got over it okay. And I decided then—no more. He needs to breathe. I need to breathe. We're stifling each other. I told him on the way home. He'll sulk around tonight, and tomorrow he'll be calling and writing and hounding me, but this time it's over. Finished! Kaput!"

The following week, she started going around with Bruce Robbins. Gary met me in school or called me on the phone. He wanted me to tell him what she was doing and what she said about him. I told him to be patient, that it would blow over as it always had in the past. He said he thought there was a limit to his patience. He also said he was going out with Morgan Jennings, and that he thought she was a beautiful girl and much nicer than Cass.

In March, Cass got accepted into Harvard. The next day, she and Gary came home from school together, hand in hand. They stayed in her room the whole afternoon, and Mom complained. But she invited him for dinner that night and even pulled a lemon cake out of the freezer.

6

I sewed.

In January, I had made myself a two-piece wool challis dress with pearl buttons on the front and a scalloped collar.

In February, I had made a blue wool blazer trimmed with red braid and lined in red taffeta. I matched it with a pleated wool skirt, and even Dad said he thought I looked great.

In March, I began looking at fashion magazines and learning names like Saint Laurent, Oscar de la Renta and Bill Blass. I threw away my tacky green shirred dress, and I offered to make my mother a fashionable silk dress with a matching lined jacket.

"When would I wear such a thing?" Mom said. "I never go anywhere."

"Well, maybe if you and Dad go out to dinner one night . . ."

"You mean to the Chinese restaurant or for pizza?"

"I saw this beautiful fabric at Britex," I told her, "on sale for just a fraction of its cost—a beautiful deep blue silk from China. It would look wonderful on you, Mom. It would bring out the blue in your eyes."

"Who's interested in the blue of my eyes?"

For a change, Cass agreed with me. "Listen, Mom, your twentieth anniversary's coming up in April. That's special. Dad and you should really go out to a fancy restaurant and have a wild time. I tell you what—that can be Penny's and my gift to you. If Penny will make the dress, I'll buy the material."

Mom said no. And Dad mumbled something about being busy and never fussing over wedding anniversaries anyway.

Cass insisted. She came with me to Britex, made a face over the beautiful deep blue silk I wanted to buy and instead picked out a vivid turquoise silk, also on sale.

"She'll never wear a dress that color," I protested.

Cass didn't like my choice of a pattern either—an understated, slim dress with a cowl neckline and a long jacket.

"Too blah," Cass said. "She needs something to shake her up a little." She flipped through the pattern book and paused over a picture of a sultry-looking model in a sexy dress with narrow shoulder straps, a low blouson bodice and a shaped, overlapping front hemline. It had a skimpy, matching sleeveless jacket.

"Can you make this?" Cass asked.

"Well, sure," I told her, "but that's not appropriate for Mom. She's over forty years old. She'll never wear a dress like that."

"She'll wear it," Cass said. "Jane Fonda's nearly fifty, and Joan Collins is over fifty. Forty's not so old, and Mom's figure is still pretty good."

Mom said, "Absolutely not! That dress is indecent. I wouldn't be seen dead in a dress like that. And that material is much too flashy."

"It's time you changed your image," Cass said. "You're only forty, but you look older than Gary's mother, and she's nearly fifty."

Mom took a deep breath and studied the pattern. "I think I'd feel cold in a dress like that," she said finally. "You know I have a touch of arthritis in my shoulders."

"You can put the jacket on if you're cold."

"But the jacket doesn't have sleeves."

"You can wear gloves. Come on, Mom, give Dad a thrill. Put a little romance back in your life."

Mom looked up and blinked. "Maybe I'd better show it to him first and see what he thinks."

"No, you don't, Mom. We'll surprise Dad. It will be like a second honeymoon. As a matter of fact, why don't you and Dad stay out that night? Treat yourself good for a change. We'll book you a room at the Stanford Court."

"The Stanford Court," Mom shrieked. "Do you know how much that costs?"

"And you can have dinner at Fournou's Ovens—or maybe that new hotel south of Market with the fantastic French chef. Just leave it to me, Mom. I'll make all the reservations. You and Dad will only have to pay."

As usual, when Cass made up her mind, all opposition crumbled. For me, it was wonderful having her as an ally. She supervised the fittings, tugging down on the bodice every time Mom tried to pull it up. She argued Dad into canceling his appointments for the evening of the anniversary and taking the next day off as well.

"But what will we do?" Dad asked.

"If you don't know after twenty years of marriage," Cass told him, "we'll have to give you up as a lost cause. But if everything else fails, you can take a boat ride out to Alcatraz."

I worked on Mom's dress for nearly a whole week.

The jacket needed to be redone because I felt it didn't lie right around the neck.

"Who's going to notice?" Mom said. "And for the one time I'll wear it, Penny, you don't have to bother."

"I don't mind," I told her. "And this won't be the last time. You'll see, Mom. This will only be the beginning."

As the week progressed, Mom seemed to get caught up in the excitement. She bought herself a new pair of black sandals, and on the anniversary day she spent the afternoon in the beauty salon, coming home with a new short, flippy hairdo and bright red fingernails.

"Wowie!" Cass grinned when she saw the fingernails. "There won't be any stopping you now, Mom."

Cass saw to it that Dad wore his blue suit, a white shirt and the best tie she could find. "We really should have done a little more rehabilitation on you, Dad," she told him. "But we'll focus on you next time around." She pulled him away from his desk, handed him a box with a purple orchid for Mom and stationed him in the living room while I adjusted the dress on Mom.

When Mom took one final look at herself in the full-length mirror in her bedroom, she sucked in her breath and smiled. She looked wonderful—glamorous, young and very pretty. The color leaped into her face and down her neck.

I smoothed one shoulder where the strap buckled just a bit, and I yanked at the hem and told her to stand up straight. She didn't hear me. She was too enchanted with her image in the mirror.

Cass clapped her hands together when she saw Mom coming down the stairs. "God, Mom," she said, "you're gorgeous. And that dress—wow—Dad will have to fight off any guy that sees you in it."

Mom didn't say anything. She didn't say anything about the arthritis in her shoulders or that the bodice was indecent. She just grinned at Dad and gave a little giggle.

"Well," Dad said, "well . . ." And he handed her the orchid.

"Well," I said to Cass, after they'd gone. "What do you think?"

"I think," Cass said, "that the two of them never should have married. It was fun playing with them the way we did, but I'm exhausted and way behind in my work. Chances are, it won't make any difference anyway."

"Don't say that, Cass," I pleaded. "Mom looked gorgeous, and I think Dad was really surprised when he saw her. I think they'll have a great time. I think they'll have fun. I really do. Don't you, Cass? Don't you think they'll have fun?"

"I sure hope so," she said. "It's going to cost them enough."

She looked at her watch. "Nearly seven," she said. "I told Gary I'd call him after they left. We're going to grab a hamburger at McDonald's and then go over to the main library. I need some books on Ezra Pound for my American poetry class. Gary can go and look at *Playboy* magazines while I'm busy."

"Oh," I said. "You're going out."

I didn't want the good feeling between us to end. We had worked together for weeks, it seemed, getting Mom ready for her big night. Now Cass was going off with Gary, busy on her own concerns, and I felt empty and alone.

"I need to get going on that report. I've been wasting my time these past couple of weeks." She studied my face. "Don't you have any schoolwork to do?"

"No," I lied. "I'm all caught up."

I wasn't. I never was caught up in school. I was weeks behind in algebra, and I also had a book report due for English on a book I hadn't even read.

"Do you want to come along with us?" Cass said. "We'll all have hamburgers, and then you can look at *Seventeen* or whatever highbrow magazine you like, while Gary reads *Playboy* and I get my work done. Would you like that, Penny?"

"Oh, yes, Cass," I said. "I'm ready. I'll just get my jacket. I'm ready."

Cass started talking again about how I needed some new friends and some other interests, but I didn't care. I was so happy she was letting me come with her and Gary, it didn't matter to me what she said.

Gary and I sat in the periodical room of the library while we waited for Cass to pick up her books on Ezra Pound. We had magazines in front of us, but at first neither of us looked at them. I told him about Mom and Dad and how Cass had masterminded the whole thing.

"Shh!" a man next to Gary said.

For a little while, we both flipped through our magazines. I had a copy of *Vogue* in front of me and was wondering how I would look in a white Bill Blass dress with huge shoulders when Gary started talking again. He told me that he would be working in a new computer store in Daly City this summer, and maybe, if they liked him, he might stay on in the fall and take some computer courses at City College.

"Will you kids shut up!" said the man in a loud, cranky voice.

"Take it easy, mister," Gary told him. But then the librarian came over and said if we were going to talk, we should leave.

"Never mind, Baby Sister," Gary said, standing up and making a lot of noise scraping his chair back and forth. "We'll go someplace else."

So we sat on the stairs up on the third floor and talked. Gary said he was very happy. He said Cass had admitted that she cared for him and that she had missed him during the time they had broken off.

"See!" I said. "Didn't I tell you to be patient?"

"Yes, you did, Baby Sister." He reached over and took my hand. "You're really the best friend I've got."

"Well," I said, "well . . ."

He kept holding my hand. I didn't want to move. I wanted to freeze time and stay there on the library steps forever with Gary holding my hand.

"It's a funny thing . . ." Gary began to say. But then two girls came up the stairs. They saw us sitting there, holding hands, and one of them started giggling. Gary dropped my hand and moved away from me.

"What were you saying?" I asked.

"When?"

"Before. You said, 'It's a funny thing . . .' and then the girls came up the stairs."

Gary wrinkled up his face. "I don't remember."

"Oh, well, it doesn't matter. You were saying how Cass said she really cared for you, and I said how I told you to be patient and you . . ."

"Oh, yeah!" He nodded up and down and smiled. Gary's smile lifts up his cheekbones and makes his blue eyes slant. He was always the most handsome boy in the whole world, even if the cowlick at the back of his head grew larger and larger as each day passed. "She's really never been sweeter. She's like the way she was when we first started going around together. I wish . . . I wish . . ." He stopped smiling. His eyes unslanted, and his cheekbones dropped.

"What do you wish, Gary?"

"I just wish she weren't going so far away."

"Me too," I said. "I can't stand thinking about it."

"I mean," Gary said, "I know she's smart. Everybody knows that. But she doesn't have to go to Harvard. She got into Stanford. That's a great school, and it's less than an hour away. Or Berkeley. She got in there too, and this kid I was talking to in my judo class was telling me a lot of people think it's the best school in the country. She could go to Berkeley."

"I think so too," I said. "If she went to Berkeley, she could even live at home."

"That's right," Gary said. "Your folks aren't loaded. It would be a lot easier for them financially if she went to Berkeley and lived at home."

"Well, Harvard is giving her a big scholarship," I said. "But I know she hasn't sent back the acceptance forms to either Berkeley or Stanford."

"No?" Gary said. "Are you sure?"

Well, yes, I was sure, but I couldn't tell him why. Only yesterday I had been prowling around in her room. All the college acceptance letters lay on her desk, entwined with other letters, photos, dirty socks and half a bag of peanuts. But she was definitely going to Harvard. I knew that for sure.

Hurry April! Hurry May! June! July! August! I am choking in this place.

"I'm sure," I said.

"But, maybe there's still a chance she won't go to Harvard. Maybe she's not absolutely sure. What do you think, Penny?"

I looked at his loving face, and I began to feel frightened for him. She'll always come back to him, I told myself. Tell him that she'll always come back. Tell him to be patient.

"Gary," I said, "she's definitely going to Harvard. That's settled, so don't get your hopes up. She won't change her mind."

I was looking at my fingernails now. I didn't want to see his face. I needed a nail file. There was dirt under my middle fingernail, and the cuticle of my pinky had climbed up too high over the nail.

"Oh!"

"But you'll still have a lot of time together before she goes," I said, smoothing the cuticle with my fingers. "You have the rest of the term and the prom and the whole summer."

"Yeah," he said. "But it will go fast."

"And you'll write to each other."

"Yeah."

"And she'll be home for Christmas. Time always goes fast in the fall." I was jabbering away now. "There's Columbus Day and Halloween and Thanksgiving. You'll see. It will go fast. Just be patient."

He didn't say anything, so I took a deep breath and began desperately to talk about the senior prom. I told him I wanted to make Cass's dress. Maybe this time she would consider wearing a gown, and then he could wear a tux, and they would really look like two people going to a prom. He brightened up, and I told him how I had seen two gorgeous patterns for prom dresses. One

54

was a billowy, flouncy sort of Victorian dress that could be made in pink chiffon, and the other was a Laura Ashley pattern that could be done in white eyelet with blue ribbons. He, of course, I said, could wear a white tux or one that coordinated with Cass's gown.

That cheered him up. He forgot all about Cass's departure, and by the time she found us, we were deep in happy plans for her senior prom.

At first, Cass said no.

"But why, Cass? I'll make you any kind of dress you like, and it will cost only a fraction of what you'd pay in the stores."

"Stop talking like that, Penny," she snapped. "I hate it when you talk like that. Just leave me alone. I don't want you sewing for me."

"Why not?" I insisted. "You never let me make anything for you. Why not?"

She kept saying no. Mom took my part and ended up shouting at Cass and calling her selfish. Dad, of course, didn't say anything to her, but he didn't stick up for her either. And Gary—Gary was on my side all the way.

"She wants us to wear matching guerrilla outfits," he said bitterly. "Boots and old camouflage pants and helmets. Why does she always have to be different from everybody else? Why can't we look like other people for a change?"

"There was this gorgeous grape-colored georgette at Britex," I told him. "Just think how it would look with her eyes and hair. And I saw a pattern, a designer pattern, with filmy sleeves and a layered skirt."

"I want to wear a tux," Gary said.

"Gary wants to wear a tux," I told Cass.

"Bug off," she said to me. Cass was working on a

report for school—an analysis of the French court during the time of Cardinal Richelieu. "I love history," she murmured. "Especially European history. I love the way nothing ever works out the way it should. It's like a jigsaw puzzle that keeps falling apart in different ways."

"Why?" I insisted. "Why won't you let me make you a dress? Just tell me why."

Cass took all the pages of her report and bounced them up and down on her messy desk. "This is my final report for high school," she said dreamily. "No more real work now until I graduate. It's a whole part of my life that's ending."

"Why, Cass, why?"

She put her report in a folder, then smiled at me. She was in a good mood. "I don't know, Penny. It doesn't feel right. It doesn't feel like me."

"What doesn't?

"Having you make me a dress. Picking out a pattern and material. Having you fit it on with pins in your mouth while I turn around in front of a mirror. Besides, I think it would be fun if Gary and I went over to the secondhand shop on the Presidio and bought some old army camouflage clothes."

"Gary wants to wear a tux. You never think of him. You're going away, and the least you can do is leave him with some happy memories."

"Penny," Cass said between her teeth, "sometimes you sound like a character from one of your soaps. I hate it when you sound like that."

"Or me," I said. "Don't you ever think of me? What I want? You keep saying I need to find myself. Well, I've found myself. I want to sew. I want to sew something for you because I can do it well. It's the only thing I can do well. You're always doing things for me, and now I want to do something for you. You're going away, Cass, and I want to make you a prom dress. Like I made that dress for Mom's anniversary. You went along with that, Cass. You know you did."

"Yes, I did," Cass admitted, "and I'm sorry I did because what good did it do? Mom is back to complaining full time, and we hardly ever see Dad. And the dress is just hanging in the closet."

"But she was happy that night when she wore it, Cass. I want to make you happy too. Please, Cass! Please let me make you happy!"

Finally, she said yes. She gave a squeezed kind of laugh and said, "Okay, Penny, this prom is for you."

When he heard, Gary picked me up, spun me around and gave me a long, hard kiss on my mouth. It was the first time he had ever kissed me like that.

Cass didn't care for any of the patterns I showed her. She said no to all the dresses with lace, flounces or ruffles. Instead, she picked a tight-fitting sleeveless dress that looped over one shoulder. It had a slit that came up to her thigh and seemed entirely inappropriate for a prom.

"It's not appropriate for a prom," I told her. "You need a full skirt, so when you dance the skirt can swirl around."

"Not the way Gary and I dance," Cass said. "Look, you said I can have any dress I want. That's the one I want."

But if I didn't approve of the pattern Cass had selected, I disapproved even more of the color of the fabric.

"Black! Cass, you're not going to a funeral. You're going to a prom. You should pick white or some kind of pastel color."

"It's what I want," she said.

I tried to get Gary to intercede but he was so delighted that he could wear a tux and didn't have to go in old army clothes that he preferred not to rock the boat.

"Leave her alone," he said, "or she might change her mind."

Cass wrote in her diary:

I don't know why, but I feel like screaming every time Penny gets started on the prom dress. Why am I going in the first place? Last year I was only a junior, and I was curious. Even then, I wasn't going to run with the herd, which was why we dressed up in funny clothes. If I had decided not to go, this whole business over the prom dress never would have come up. Now it's too late. She's making me a dress, and I hate the whole thought of it. I won't be Little Bo Peep for her or Gary or anybody else. I'm trying to sabotage the whole thing. Why? Why am I going in black just to spite her? Why can't I let her have pleasure out of making a dress for me? Why? Why? Why? There is something else going on here that I don't really understand.

Every time I fitted the dress on her, she struggled inside of it as if I was hurting her.

"Did I stick you with a pin, Cass?"

"No, no. It's all right."

"Well, try to stand still. I can't get this waist right if you keep moving around."

The material, a heavy taffeta moiré, squeaked as she moved inside of it.

"Gary doesn't know whether to get a white or a black tux," I told her as I adjusted a dart in the back.

Cass shrugged.

"I think a white tux is more summery, but of course if you're wearing black, I suppose it would make more sense if he wore a black tux."

"Whatever he likes," Cass said impatiently. "And for God's sake, Penny, hurry it up. You keep making me try this thing on a million times a day. I'm sick of it. I never would have said yes if I'd known how much time this was going to take. I think you're doing it on purpose."

"You didn't give me much time." I raised up the waist seam a little. "The prom is next week. Cass, you need to make up your mind about the flowers. Gary thought a wristlet of white roses, but I wondered if one white orchid . . ."

"Stop it!" Cass yelled. "Stop talking about the dumb prom. I'm sorry I ever got into this."

"Okay, okay, Cass. Calm down. Just one more thing, and we're through. Would you like me to make you a white tulle shawl? I could sew on some black pearls or even some black sequins if you prefer."

I thought she was going to explode. She pulled off the dress, flung it at me and looked as if she would punch me with her clenched fists. I had to rebaste one underarm seam and the darts in the back, but I did end up making her a white tulle shawl trimmed with black sequins.

I surrender. I quit the field. She wins. Let her enjoy. I'm too exhausted to continue.

The night of the prom, Gary brought her a wristlet of three tiny white orchids. I opened the door and let him in. He looked magnificent in his black tuxedo, and very happy.

60

"Is she ready?" he whispered.

"Nearly. Just sit down a few minutes and talk to Dad. I'll go up and help her."

Cass was sitting on her bed, still in her slip. The dress was hanging up on the closet door where I'd hung it earlier in the day.

"Come on, Cass. Gary's waiting. Here, let me help you."

She looked tired. I got her up, slipped the dress over her head, zipped it up, smoothed it down the back and stood her in front of the mirror.

"Come on, Cass, fix your hair. Put on some makeup."

I buzzed and bustled around her while she slowly did what I told her to do. Her hair hung around her face in its usual wet curls, but I handed her lipstick and eye makeup, and she began applying them.

Mom came into the room. "Cass, are you nearly ready? Oh . . ." Mom cocked her head to one side and examined Cass. "Oh—it's beautiful, Cass, and it fits you perfectly. Will you just look at that fit. Penny, you've really got magic fingers. I'll tell you the truth, Cass. I didn't like that pattern or the material, but Penny has really made you look stunning."

Cass stood in front of the full-length mirror on her closet door and looked at herself. She was beautiful, more beautiful than any of the models on any of the patterns in the Vogue pattern book, I thought. Her face was very pale, and her green yellow eyes looked enormous under her green yellow hair, set off by the black of her dress. She wasn't smiling. Her face had almost a sullen, angry look that matched the dress perfectly.

"No jewelry?" Mom asked.

Cass shook her head.

"I don't know," Mom said. "If you promise to be careful, you can wear my pearls or even that crystal necklace. What do you think, Penny? A little something around the neck? Don't you think it looks too severe this way?"

"No jewelry," Cass said.

"I think she's right, Mom," I said. "And besides, she'll have the flowers on her wrist and, of course, the tulle shawl."

"But just a little jewelry. How about a pin? My rhinestone rose pin up there at the shoulder?"

"No, Mom." I led Cass to the door. "I think she looks perfect just the way she is."

"Oh, well, if you really think so. . . . But, Cass, aren't you going to thank Penny? She's been working day and night for you. Aren't you going to tell her thank you?"

"Thank you," Cass said over her shoulder, without looking at me, as she moved downstairs.

She got smashed that night.

I heard them come in at about four in the morning, and I hurried downstairs. Gary was carrying her through the door. He was pretty loaded himself, but he was grinning.

"Man!" he said. "What a night! What a night!"

Between us, we carried her up the stairs and laid her down on the bed. The first thing I noticed was that the dress was ruined. There were stains all over the front, and a huge tear right in the center of the skirt.

"What a night!" Gary chuckled and dropped down on the bed next to her. She was sleeping, a peaceful look on her face. He picked up one of her limp hands and stroked it.

"I never saw her like this before. She was really the life of the party. Everybody wanted to be near her, but I didn't mind. She was so gorgeous—she made all the other girls look like cows in their silly little dresses. She was a wild one, I tell you, but she always came back looking for me. All night long, she had a million different guys after her, but she always kept calling for me. 'Gary! Gary! Gary!'" He planted a loud, drunken kiss on her forehead. "My darling girl—she needs me. And I was there. When she passed out, I caught her. She knew I'd be there."

"You're drunk," I snapped at him. "Look what she did to her dress. How could you let her ruin her dress?"

"What? What?" Gary blinked.

"Just look at these stains. And this rip. I won't be able to fix it."

"It's not my fault," Gary said. "She kept spilling things, and somebody stepped on her dress while she was dancing. It wasn't me, Baby Sister. It's not my fault."

"It's disgusting," I cried. "You're so drunk, it's a miracle you didn't crack up the car. You could have killed Cass, you idiot. How could you get so drunk? I thought you had better sense than that."

His head began wobbling, and before I had finished talking, he just flopped down on the bed next to Cass. I left them there together. He obviously was in no shape to drive home, and I was too angry to want to protect them from Mom's anger when she found them there the next morning.

But Mom didn't get angry. "Listen," she said, "I was young once too."

"They were both stinking drunk, Mom. They could have gotten themselves killed."

"Oh, it probably wasn't as bad as that, Penny. You know Cass never really drinks. I have to say that for her. And Gary—well, he's always dependable."

"You didn't see them, Mom. Cass had passed out, and Gary was too drunk to go home."

"Shh! Don't yell so loud. Let them sleep for now. I'll talk to them later."

"And she ruined the dress," I said, beginning to cry. "You didn't see the dress, Mom. It has a big tear in the skirt and stains all over the front. It's ruined."

Mom put her arms around me. "She really is a slob, Penny. You know that. It doesn't pay making her beautiful things." She patted my cheek, and I lay my head on her shoulder. "But I know she must have had a wonderful night, and I'm sure your dress made it really special for her."

"Do you think so, Mom? Really?"

"Of course I do." Mom kissed me and gave me another pat on the cheek.

"Don't say so if you don't think so, Mom. Do you really think she liked the dress? She never said she liked it."

"I'm sure she loved it. You know Cass. She doesn't act like other people, but she'll never do what she doesn't want to do. You can be sure of that. She never would have worn the dress if she didn't love it. And how could she not love it?"

"Well, she didn't want me to make it, Mom. You remember. I think maybe she really hated it."

"No, no, no!" Mom said. "You're too sensitive,

Penny, when it comes to Cass. Listen to me. It's a crying shame that the dress is ruined, but I'm sure you gave her a night she'll always remember. She'll have happy memories as long as she lives, because of you."

"And Gary too," I said.

8

That summer, Cass went out of her way to be kind. To me, to Gary and even to my parents. She was kind to everybody.

The final act. Before the curtain rings down. It's going faster than I had hoped. I do love them all, and I can't wait to leave.

She even apologized to me over the dress and seemed genuinely unhappy when I said it was impossible to fix. When she saw my final marks—all C's and C−'s except for a D in English—I was amazed at her self-control.

Those who can, can. Those who can't . . . Maybe Penny just can't. It's hard to believe there's as little upstairs as there seems to be. All she wants to do is sew. Most of the things she makes are dull copies of what's supposed to be fashionable. She is the one person who will suffer when I go. At least I've been a thorn in her side, refusing to allow her to sink into complacency. But time is running out. And Gary? Poor Gary. Poor, darling Gary. He will be better off when I go, but in the meantime . . .

In the meantime, Gary was content. All of us had jobs that summer, he in the computer store, Cass for a lawyer, and I—lucky me—I had been hired at Britex, on the second floor, where the cottons are. I swam in the colors and designs. I stroked and smoothed the bolts of fabrics as I walked up and down the aisles. I threw myself into the sewing projects of customers, recommending this or that fabric as if it were a dear and special friend. After only a few weeks, the boss offered me a part-time job once school started in the fall.

Cass had managed to get a job in the office of a famous civil rights lawyer. He was a friend of one of her teachers, who had given her a glowing recommendation.

"He's a dirty old man," Cass said, laughing. "I wouldn't want to meet him behind the file cabinet, but what's a little squeeze or pinch compared to all the noble causes he stands up for? And very often he doesn't even get paid, according to his secretary."

Cass thought she might like to go into international law.

"There's a lot of junk you have to memorize," she said, "and some of the teachers at law school, I understand, are really sadistic. But once you're through, you've got power to really do good in this world. You can make a difference with your life."

I showed her some ivory and green striped linen I had picked up at a steal.

"If you like, Cass, I can make you a skirt and matching jacket to wear when you go East. Oversized blazers are in this year, and they're really comfortable."

Cass pushed the fabric away. "Don't you want your life to mean anything, Penny? Don't you want to feel when you're old that you've made a difference in the world?"

"Well, sure," I said. "I want to make people I care about happy. I want to be happy too and have fun."

Cass said thank you, but she didn't need any more clothes. Later, she wrote in her diary:

> *I'm not perfect. I'm arrogant, inconsiderate and intolerant. But I want my life to expand outside of myself. I want my work to be more than me. There's so much to do and only one short life to do it in.*

That summer, I made myself a one-piece bathing suit out of a shimmery pale gold stretch nylon with a co-ordinating yellow and white beach jacket. Gary and Cass let me come along with them one Sunday when they drove out to Lake Anza.

"Why don't you bring along a friend?" Cass said.

"Who?"

"I don't know who. Isn't there any guy you could ask?"

"You know there isn't. They don't like me. You know that."

"Okay, okay. How about a girlfriend?"

"Who?"

"Are you starting that all over again? You sound like a broken record."

"There's no point in asking Catherine. She never wears a bathing suit because her thighs are so heavy."

Cass snorted. "Isn't there anybody else?"

"Well . . . oh, I know. There's a girl—Roseanne—she works with me at Britex, but downstairs in silks and woolens. I meet her on the bus a lot on the way to work, and yesterday she asked me to have lunch with her."

"Good. Call her up. Call anybody up."

Roseanne came. It turned out she was about Cass and Gary's age and had also just graduated from high school. She was planning to work a year or so and then go back to school.

"What are you interested in?" Cass asked while we were driving over to Berkeley.

"Pardon?"

"What are you going to study in school?"

"Oh. I think I'll go into dental hygiene. My brother's girlfriend is a dental hygienist, and she makes good money. She can also arrange her hours any way she likes."

Cass remained silent, but Gary began talking about how he hated dentists, and soon the three of us were laughing and comparing notes about dentists we had all known and hated.

Roseanne had made her bathing suit too. She was a good sewer but not as good as me. Her bathing suit, a skimpy, black bikini with crisscross tapes on each side, bunched up more than it should have in the front. But her figure was good—tall, slim and very tanned except underneath the crisscrosses. As soon as we'd spread our blankets down on the beach, Roseanne pulled out a bottle of suntan lotion and began smoothing it all over her body.

"Why don't you wait until we come out of the water?" Cass said. She pulled off her jeans and shirt and stood there in an old white one-piece bathing suit that had stretched out of shape. It pulled across her bust and around her butt.

"No," Roseanne said, eyeing Cass's suit. "I don't usually swim. I'll just lie here in the sun and work on my tan."

Cass gave the bottom of her suit a tug and yanked at Gary's arm. "Let's go, Gary."

"Just wait a second. I've got to get my shoes off."

She turned to me. "Are you ready, Penny?"

"No. I don't think I'm going to swim today, Cass. I feel a cold coming on. Maybe I'll just sit here in the sun."

I stepped out of my pants and unbuttoned my shirt. Roseanne's eyes fixed themselves on me. I could feel them moving up and down my new suit with what I imagined was admiration and envy.

Cass said in a disgusted voice, "You mean you're going to sit around here all day showing off your new suit?"

"It's gorgeous!" Roseanne explained. "What pattern was that?"

"Oh—just a Butterick," I told her lightly. "Nothing fancy."

"And that fabric! What a color!"

"Let's go," Cass said to Gary, "before I throw up."

Roseanne took her eyes off my suit to survey Cass's retreating back. Cass is a tall girl with a statuesque figure. She's solid all around, but she did seem to be bursting out of her suit.

"She could stand a size larger," Roseanne announced gently.

"I know, I know," I said, feeling guilty. "She doesn't care about clothes."

"She'd look a lot nicer," Roseanne continued, "if she took a little better care of herself."

"She looks gorgeous as is," I bristled. "She's always had more guys after her than she could handle."

Roseanne looked up at me and smiled. "Is he—Gary—her boyfriend, or are they just friends?"

"He's her boyfriend," I said firmly.

Roseanne kept smiling. She handed me her bottle of suntan lotion and said I should try some. Then she began asking me questions about my suit and the matching beach jacket. She couldn't praise them enough.

"Nice girl," Gary said, after we dropped her off.

"I don't think so," Cass said.

"Why not?" I demanded. "Because she's not going on to college? Because she's not ambitious?"

"No," Cass said. "Because she reminds me of a wolf. She's always looking at you like she wants to tear you apart. Even while she was eating her sandwich, her eyes kept darting around, looking at everybody else's sandwich like she'd like to eat them too."

"I thought she was nice," Gary insisted.

"You would," Cass said. "She kept looking you over like she wouldn't mind getting a bite of you too. Ugh! I didn't like her."

"I think you're jealous," Gary said happily.

"I sure am." Cass lay her head on his shoulder. "I don't want you looking at anybody else, and I don't want anybody looking at you."

She made him very happy that summer. Any free time she had, she spent with him.

"She's hardly reading," Gary said. "I think school makes her nervous. She always has to get A's in everything. But now that she's all finished, she can really relax. And she wants to be with me all the free time she has. That's what she told me."

Gary said he wanted to marry Cass and would be willing to wait a couple of years, but she just laughed when he told her.

"She'll change her mind," I told him. "Just be patient."

I was setting the table in the dining room, and Gary was helping me. Cass hadn't returned home from work yet, but Mom had invited Gary to stay for dinner. Gary folded the napkins into triangles, and I followed after him, changing them into rectangles.

"She could still finish school," Gary said. "I could go wherever she is and find a job."

"Sure you could."

"She says we're both too young to even think about getting married," Gary said glumly. "Maybe she is, but I've been thinking about marrying her since I was thirteen."

"I'll make her wedding gown," I told him. "There's a beautiful designer gown in the new Vogue pattern book. It has a keyhole neckline, a lace bodice with little seed pearls and modified leg-of-mutton sleeves."

"She'd ruin it," Gary said. "She always ruins her dresses."

"I wouldn't care," I told him. "As long as it made you both happy—as long as you had that one perfect day."

Gary sighed. "I don't know, Baby Sister. I don't know."

"Just be patient."

It was a happy summer for all of us, but as the days passed, as the time grew closer and closer, I began feeling frightened.

"I'm scared," I told Mom. "I'm scared of what it will be like when she's gone."

Mom was ironing some of Cass's blouses, even though Cass kept telling her not to bother, that she could wear them unironed. "It will be a lot easier for me, I can tell you that. I won't have to clean her room or look after her clothes. Did you see the bathroom this morning? When she showers, the whole floor gets wet. I have to mop up after her every time she takes a shower."

I knew Mom was frightened too.

Dad kept saying how proud he was of Cass and how good it would be for her to go to such a prestigious school and how important for her to make all the contacts she'd need.

"But aren't you going to miss her, Dad?"

"Miss her? Well . . . well . . ." He started talking about how parents had to get used to the idea of their kids growing up and leaving them. That parents should never try to stop their children from going, and that, yes, he would miss her. But, of course, she would be coming home for Christmas and summers, and maybe he would go East in March.

"What for?" Mom demanded. "Why will you be going East in March?"

"Oh—there's going to be a national conference of psychologists in Boston in March."

"But you never go to conferences."

"Well, I might this time."

"I'll go too. We'll both go."

"And what about me?" I said. "If the two of you are going to see Cass, why shouldn't I go too?"

All of us were terrified.

Cass and I had one last, wonderful night together, the two of us, just before she left. She came in late, about two in the morning, and called me. "Penny, Penny, are you up?" I jumped right out of bed and followed her into her bedroom. I looked around at the lovely jumble and at Cass sitting up in the middle of her messy bed. She was grinning at me, her lamp throwing lights and shadows on her green yellow hair and eyes.

"I'm scared," she said, still smiling.

"Me too. Me too," I cried, flinging myself down beside her. "Don't go, Cass. Stay here! Stay with me and with Gary! It's not too late to change your mind."

I buried my face in her neck and smelled the sweaty, unwashed comforting smell of her hair. She kissed my head and patted my back. "We'll both get over it, Penny," she said. "It's time."

We talked for hours. She said if ever I was really unhappy or troubled I should call her. She was always there for me. She said if she had ever made me feel bad—if she had ever said anything that hurt me—she was sorry. She said she loved me very much, would always love me and would always be there if I needed her.

I told her that I was going to miss her so much I didn't know if I could manage. I told her she made my life and Mom's life and Dad's life and Gary's life wonderful—just because she was a part of it.

We both cried, and then we fell asleep together, and the next thing, it was morning, and Mom was waking us up and saying today was the day.

Later, after Cass had left, I came into her room, looking for the diary. It was gone. She had taken it with her. I sat there on her bed, and I thought I might die.

Mom came in with the vacuum cleaner.

"I feel like I'm dying," I told her.

"You'll live." Mom plugged in the vacuum cord. "We all will. The best way to get your mind off your troubles is work. Why don't you pull off the sheets on Cass's bed and put up a laundry. I'm going to vacuum, and later you can help me sort through all those papers on her desk. Then you can hang up her clothes. It will take us days and days to straighten up in here. But this time, at least until Christmas, it will stay straightened up."

9

October 3

Dear Penny,

I promised you I would write, so here goes. Does it seem strange to be receiving a letter from me? This must be the first I've written to you. Postcards from camp don't count. I'm really depending on you to write long, newsy letters telling me everything that's happening back home. To my surprise, I'm a lot more homesick than I expected.

School is exciting. I like my classes and am beginning to feel more comfortable with my fellow students. Most of them are Eastern and different. How? More formal, more serious and a lot more competitive. I'm still used to the California model. But it will be good for me to try out against the genuine article. I don't think anybody takes me seriously—yet. They think I'm one of those flaky Californians. I know my roommate is amazed at the way I dress. She's preppy—plaid skirts, blazers and crisp little button-down shirts. The other morning, we had classes at the same time, and she suggested we have breakfast and walk across the campus together. "Fine with me," I said, and then she said she'd wait until I got dressed. "I am dressed," I told her. That day, I was wearing a pair of lavender sweatpants, sandals and a yellow tank top. But I like her. She lives in New York City—on the East Side. That's supposed to make a difference. I guess she's a snob, but why shouldn't she be? She's smart and good-looking, and

76

if I can get her to laugh a little more, I think we'll get along fine.

The East feels different from the West. Aside from the people, the buildings are brick and stone instead of wood and stucco. There's a snap in the air, even though the days are still pretty warm, and some of the leaves are beginning to fall from the big, old trees on the campus. The school is lovely— old, dignified and sort of benign.

But I still think of all of you back home. I see Dad retreating behind his newspaper, Mom fussing over something, and you, my darling, little baby sister, I see you sitting right down and writing me a long, newsy letter, bringing me up to date on how everybody is and how much you all miss me. Write soon!

Lots of love,
Cass

P.S. And tell me how Gary is. He's written me twelve letters and seven postcards since I left home, so I don't really need to ask. But I want another partial opinion.

P.P.S. And tell me who your teachers are this term, what courses you're enjoying and when you'll be taking the P.S.A.T.'s. Also, of course, if there are any interesting males in your life.

I wrote to Cass the same day. I didn't say much about school, because there wasn't much to say. I told her the names of all my teachers, said I wasn't enjoying any of the courses and did not plan on taking the P.S.A.T.'s. There weren't any males in my life, and I told her that too. Maybe she was kidding when she said I should tell her how much we all missed her, but I spent most of the letter doing just that.

I didn't tell her that her room was like a ghost room and that I tiptoed whenever I came into it. Mom had cleaned and scrubbed and rearranged Cass's closet so that nothing fell out when you opened the door. All her shoes were arranged in a shoe bag, and her bed was always neatly made. I would sit on it and look around me desperately. No clutter on the top of her desk. The picture of her and Gary at the junior prom (they never took one at the senior prom—Gary said he wanted to, but she refused) standing up in its place, Cass grinning out at me as I mourned her loss.

I told Cass I missed her, but it was impossible to say on paper how much. I told her I had decided to make slipcovers for the couch and old armchair in the living room, and new drapes too. I sent along swatches—a blue gray striped rayon and cotton for the couch and a lively, stylized Pennsylvania Dutch patterned cotton for the chair in reds, blues, golds and off-whites. For the drapes, I had selected another cotton and rayon blend in gold. Mom persuaded Dad that they needed to buy a new carpet for the living room.

Cass didn't comment on the swatches. She said school was going well, she was really settling into the life at Harvard, and that her roommate, Alison Jensen, had invited her home for Thanksgiving. She asked me what I was reading.

One of the arms on the slipcover for the couch gave me a little trouble, but by the middle of October I had finished.

"I don't know," I said. "It still doesn't look right."

"Maybe because the room hasn't been painted in years and the walls look kind of tacky," Mom said.

We had it painted an off-white, and then I thought the lighting fixture should be changed. Finally, the room was finished. Dad said that he liked it better the old way.

Mom exploded. "You can never stand change. If it were up to you, everything would stay exactly the same. I remember when we had to change the cracked sink in the bathroom, you carried on so, you'd think you were losing an old friend."

"It was a much stronger sink than the new one," Dad said. "But anyway, why did you buy a blue carpet? You know I don't like blue."

"Since when?" Mom demanded. "And why didn't you come shopping with Penny and me when I asked you? I asked you over and over again. But no, you were too busy."

It was good hearing them argue again. For a while right after Cass left, life had been too quiet. My parents had even nearly given up fighting.

Mom returned the rug, and this time Dad did go along with us. We picked out a cream and gold Scandinavian rug, but Dad insisted that he still didn't like the room.

"He'll get used to it," Mom said. "He'll have to."

I offered to make new drapes for the dining room, but Mom thought the old ones still had some life in them. Then I offered to make her a new quilted bedspread with matching drapes for her bedroom, but she said she thought she'd stick with the old ones.

"They go with me," she said, "a little old, a little worn, completely ordinary."

"You didn't look ordinary in that dress I made for your anniversary," I told her.

"I know," she said. "And I didn't feel ordinary either."

"But you never wear it."

"I have no occasion to wear it."

"You can make an occasion. Get Dad to take you out and go someplace you can wear the dress. He liked the dress, didn't he? I'm sure he liked the dress."

"I doubt if he even noticed it." Mom hesitated. "There is something though, Penny, I'd like to talk to you about." She had an embarrassed smile on her face. "It's just that there's not enough to do around here since—well, since Cass left. You'll be leaving in a couple of years too."

"No, Mom, I won't be leaving. I told you I'm not going away to college."

"Well . . ." Mom's fingers began drumming on the table. She didn't look at me. "I always wanted to be home when my kids were young, but now . . . Cass is gone, and you can take care of yourself, so . . ."

"Mom, what is it?"

"It's not definite, Penny, but there's a possibility—if it's okay with you, and Dad too, of course—that I might have a job. Just a part-time job for now. Mornings until one. But she did say that after Christmas, if business improves, she might be able to use me full time. What do you think, Penny? Do you think I should take it?"

Mom turned and looked at me in a scared way, like a child who's been naughty.

"A job, Mom? You're thinking of taking a job?"

"Just part-time, Penny. I'd be able to get all my work done, and it's not like you need me every minute of the day."

"But I think it's great, Mom. You know Cass has been

at you for years to find a job. And I'll be able to make you some new clothes if you're going to work."

"It's a travel agency," Mom explained. "You know Betty Allen's sister-in-law, Rita Franklin, the one who has twins? Well, never mind. Anyway, she's just opened a travel agency. She has one full-time worker, and she said she could use me part-time. My typing isn't so good, but I think if I practiced at home . . ."

"A lot of people come into a travel agency," I said. "You'll need a suit. Every working woman needs a suit. I saw a perfect pattern in McCall's for a classic suit with a fitted jacket and a straight skirt. Maybe in a navy wool blend. And you should have some tailored dresses. I've got a lot of time these days. Nothing much is doing in school, and I'm only working eight hours a week at Britex."

Cass was delighted that Mom was working, but she didn't comment on the swatches of fabric I sent her for the suit and two dresses I made. When Mom put the suit on the first morning she started work, along with a new tailored white blouse, pearls, blue pumps, gray purse and gray tinted stockings, she looked like a real fashionable career woman.

She was waiting for me when I came home from school that day.

"Oh, Penny, I love it. And Rita says she thinks I'm going to work out just fine. You should have seen the once-over she gave me when I stepped through the door this morning. You can really feel proud, Penny. She said to me, 'Where did you get that gorgeous suit?' She couldn't believe you made it. And Penny, you know something? I didn't feel like me. I felt good and very confident. There was this client who came storming in.

81

He was really furious because somebody had given him the wrong information over the phone. He just went on and on. The other woman was out to lunch, and Rita was on the phone. So finally, I just stood up and said, 'I'm very sorry, sir, but people do make mistakes. I can promise you, though, it won't happen again.' And you know, he just stopped and looked at me. I guess I sounded very firm, like I wasn't going to take any more nonsense, but I tell you, my knees were shaking. So he said, 'Well, as long as it doesn't happen again.' And I told him very firmly, but politely, that it certainly wouldn't. When Rita heard, she said he was always difficult, but she thought I handled it very well. I tell you, Penny, wearing that suit made me feel important."

"Gray flannel," I told her. "You should have a gray flannel suit. I could make the same style, or we could try a designer pattern I noticed in the fall Vogue catalogue. They're wearing looser jackets this year, with padded shoulders and longer, fuller skirts. I could line it in a blue and gray silk paisley and make you a blouse out of the same fabric."

It was a happy time for Mom and me. We almost forgot about the hole in our lives from Cass's departure. Every day she waited for me when I got home from school. She bubbled with excitement over her new job, eager to share every detail and conversation with me.

I sewed. I made her the gray flannel suit with the matching lining and blouse, and a rose-colored wool challis dress with a coordinated vest.

"I don't know," Dad told her one evening. "We seem to be spending more money since you started work than before."

"Are you kidding?" Mom protested. "I've saved a

82

fortune on my clothes. If I had to go out and buy what Penny's sewed for me, I would have spent hundreds and hundreds—maybe a thousand dollars more than what the fabric cost me."

"But you've been buying other things. Jewlery, shoes, purses, and now you've even gotten yourself a leather briefcase. I never bought myself a leather briefcase."

"Because you're too cheap," Mom yelled. "But I'm not going to look like a slob. In my job, I have to look good."

"Yes," I chimed in, "she has to look good." Nobody seemed to hear me.

"You don't care what I look like," Mom continued. "If it were up to you, you'd keep me home all the time, barefoot and veiled in the kitchen. You want a slave, that's all you want. When it comes to male chauvinists, you're the worst."

"How can you say that?" Dad shouted. "Wasn't I the one who pushed Cass to go to Harvard? If it were up to you, she'd just go to some dinky secretarial school and be a secretary. You know I believe in careers for women. You were the one who never wanted to work. I didn't stop you."

"Yes you did," Mom yelled. "Somebody had to look after the kids and run this house, but you were never willing to do your share."

"You never let me," Dad roared.

I wrote to Cass and told her that things were falling back in place again, and that Mom and Dad were going at each other just like they always had before Mom started working.

"Sometimes," she wrote back, "I wonder why they ever married. Or are they typical of all married couples? Maybe just a little louder? I don't meet too many kids who say their parents are happy. My roomy's parents are divorced. When she's home, she lives with her mom. Her father remarried, but she says he's just as unhappy as he used to be with her mother. I wonder sometimes if marriage is just an unnatural state. Maybe I never will marry. I certainly don't want to end up like Mom and Dad."

My days speeded up because of Mom. We grew closer and closer. In a funny way, she almost stopped being my mother and I became hers. When I looked her over mornings before she left for work in one of the new outfits I'd made for her, when I straightened a collar or smoothed down a seam, when I listened to her stories about work or laughed with her when something funny happened or comforted her if a client said something unkind, I almost felt as if she were my child.

Sometimes on a Saturday, she would come downtown to meet me for lunch. I worked a whole day at Britex on Saturdays. Mom had grown more and more interested in patterns and fabrics. She'd step off the elevator, and I would proudly look around to see if anyone else noticed the smiling, well-dressed woman wearing Vogue pattern #21173 or McCall's #75426. Some of my co-workers knew that she was my mother. Roseanne knew. She didn't always recognize the exact pattern, but she knew I made nearly everything my mother wore. And she always praised me and told Mom how great she looked.

"Nice girl," Mom said. Sometimes she invited Roseanne to have lunch with us, and often we had three-way conferences to plan new dresses or skirts for Mom's wardrobe.

I took out a subscription to *Harper's Bazaar* and began browsing in department stores like I. Magnin's and Saks Fifth Avenue. I also threw out most of the clothes I had made for myself in the past and decided I needed to start all over again.

10

I saw Gary pretty often that fall. He always wanted to know what I had heard from Cass.

"Probably the same as you," I told him.

"She used to write me twice a week," Gary said. "But now I'm lucky if I hear from her twice a month."

"She's getting used to school," I said. "I think she likes her roommate too. She spent Thanksgiving weekend there, and it sounds as if she had a ball."

"Yes," he said, "that's great."

I knew he didn't mean it.

Sometimes Gary dropped by the house, and once in a while on a Saturday he'd meet me at Britex. A couple of times we had a cup of coffee while we talked about Cass.

In December, he asked me to go shopping with him and help him pick out a Christmas gift for her.

"I'm making her a new bathrobe," I told him. "It's a gorgeous pale lavender cashmere and wonderfully soft."

"I want to get her a ring," Gary said.

"A ring? I don't know, Gary. . . ."

"No, no, not an engagement ring. I'd like to give her an engagement ring, but it's no use. I know that. But how about some other kind of ring? Something . . . something special?"

"You mean like a ring with her birthstone?"

"That's it," he said. "Something like that. Something special."

Cass's birthday was in February, which meant that her birthstone was an amethyst. I knew the birthstones for each month by heart.

"Cass's birthday is in February, so her birthstone is an amethyst. Mine is in May, so I've got an emerald. Daddy's is a ruby for July, and Mom's is a garnet for January."

"Amethyst?" Gary asked. "What color is amethyst?"

"Oh—sort of a lavender. You're lucky, because it's not a precious stone like an emerald. Like my month. It won't cost you as much as if you were buying me or my dad a ring. Emeralds and rubies cost as much as diamonds."

"I've saved a couple of hundred dollars," Gary said. "I want it to be special."

Most of the stores were open on Sundays in December. We didn't have to shop for very long. Gary found it in the second jewelry store we walked into—a gold ring with an amethyst heart encircled by tiny diamond chips. The ring cost $245.

"It's very pretty," I told him. "I just hope she likes it."

Gary said he loved it, and he asked me to try it on. The ring fit perfectly—too perfectly—because Cass's fingers were thicker than mine.

"What a little hand you have," Gary said, holding my hand and examining the ring. "Your fingers are short, but Cass has long fingers. I think the ring will look beautiful on her hand."

I liked the way it looked on mine too, but I didn't

say so. I had brought one of Cass's rings along with me, and the jeweler promised to adjust the size of the new ring in time for Christmas.

It was nearly one o'clock when we left the store.

"Well, Baby Sister, where are you off to now?"

"I don't know. I could go home and work on Cass's bathrobe. It's nearly finished. I just have to do the hem. What about you? What are you doing today?"

"Nothing special. I figured it was going to take me a whole day to find a ring. I didn't plan on anything else. Actually, since Cass left, I don't generally have much to do on weekends. I jog a little, do some judo, maybe take in a movie."

"Well," I said, "I usually sew."

We were smiling and nodding at each other. I felt happy and comfortable standing there with him in front of the jewelry store where he had just bought a ring for Cass.

"I tell you what, Baby Sister," Gary said, taking my arm. "I'm going to treat you to lunch. I owe you one— you've really been a doll. You're always a doll. I guess I owe you a whole bunch of lunches. So let's really have one in style."

He took me up to the Fairmont. He said he'd always wanted to go there with Cass, but she didn't like fancy places like the Fairmont. I loved it. There was a gigantic buffet table set up in the center of the room, way up in the tower where you had a 360-degree view of the whole city. There were salads, cheeses, cold cuts, radishes cut into flowers, and a gigantic turkey and ham. You could eat as much as you liked and go back as often as you wanted.

I was too happy to eat much, but Gary went back three times.

"You eat like a bird, Baby Sister," Gary said, his mouth full of macaroni salad. "That's why you're such a little skinny thing. Cass can eat more than me, which is why she's got so much meat on her bones."

Gary told me about his job at the computer store and the courses he was taking at City College at night. He said there was a big future in computers.

Later, we wandered around some of the shops and looked at men's clothes. He said he needed some new jackets, but that he couldn't afford the kind of things he really wanted. The most successful salesman at work, he said, wore a camel's hair jacket with a pair of brown flannel pants. Customers were always impressed with class, Gary said, and when he could afford it, he planned to buy himself a camel's hair jacket.

"I'll make you one," I told him.

"What?"

"I'll make you one if you buy the fabric. I could probably get you a good price at Britex now, but maybe if we wait until after Christmas, we can get it on sale."

"You're kidding?"

It made me proud to see the way his face shone.

"No, I'm not. I've never made a man's jacket, but I don't see why I should have any problems. I've done lots of linings and pockets, and I'll have to get your measurements. But I've been wondering what to get you for Christmas, Gary, so if you'd like a camel's hair jacket, you've got it."

"I can't believe it," Gary said.

"Maybe I ought to practice on one first," I told him. "Maybe I'll make my dad a jacket for Christmas. There's some nice gray flannel on sale right now. I'll make him a jacket for Christmas just to have the experience."

Cass arrived home a few days before Christmas. Dad, Mom and I went to the airport to pick her up. As soon as she stepped into the waiting room, I could see that she had changed. Her hair no longer hung in wild, wet curls. She had cut it short, and it fluffed out around her head like a broken halo. Her clothes looked the same, but she had lost weight. Even the way she talked sounded different.

"You don't sound like you," I told her.

"Of course I sound like me."

"No, you don't. You're speaking way up in your nose and much faster."

"I'm learning Eastern." Cass laughed. "Decker says Californians sound like oranges—round and rough and without any interesting edges."

"Who's Decker?"

"Alison's brother. He's gorgeous—twenty-two and rich and handsome and crazy about me."

I could see she wasn't thinking of Gary, and it hurt me.

"Gary bought you a ring for Christmas," I told her. "It's a gold ring with an amethyst heart. Amethyst because that's your birthstone."

"Oh God!" Cass made a face. "I'm glad you told me. I only bought him a Harvard sweatshirt, so I better get him something else. What should I get him?"

"Well, I'm making him a camel's hair sport jacket for Christmas."

"Yuk!" Cass said. "Why are you doing that?"

"Because that's what he wants. You could buy him a woven tie with maybe a fancy tie clip."

"I'd rather die," Cass said.

She said yuk again when she saw the living room.

"Yuk!" she said. "What happened here?"

"I wrote you I was making slipcovers and drapes. I even sent you swatches. Mom bought a new rug, and we had the room painted."

"I never thought it would look like this."

"I liked it better the old way," Dad said. "I told them I liked it better the old way."

Cass whirled around and looked at me. "I hope you didn't touch my room."

"Well, I did think of making you a new spread and curtains, but I wasn't sure you'd like it."

"You can be sure," she said, running up the stairs. "I'd hate it, so just don't touch anything in my room!"

Cass said she was happy to be home, but she kept talking about school and her life back East.

"Alison's an old reactionary. But some other kids and I worked hard registering voters, and I also organized a demonstration against our policies in Central America. Decker says I'm a nutty, wild-eyed radical, but I don't let him intimidate me."

"You keep talking about Decker," I said. "You're not going out with him, are you?"

"Well, sure I am. He just came down one weekend after Thanksgiving. But I expect to see a lot of him when I go back."

"Gary won't like it."

Cass shrugged. "I told him before I left for school that we should both go out with different people. He knows how I feel."

"He won't like it."

Cass leaned over and kissed me. Maybe she looked and sounded different, but her hair still smelled the same. "You're a good kid, Penny, but don't worry so much about Gary. He'll be fine."

"Gary loves you," I told her. "He's going to be

hurt when he hears you're going out with Decker."

"He'd better get used to it."

Cass couldn't believe the way Mom had changed. "She's really a different person," she said to me. "Marvelous that she likes her new job so much. I just wish she talked more about her work and less about her clothes. I guess you're responsible for that."

"No, I'm not," I protested. "She has to have some new clothes. She knows that herself. You can't just wear any old rags in a travel agency."

"Why not?" Cass wanted to know. "Why do you have to worry about what you wear? You're still the same person underneath."

"No, you're not. People respect you when you're well dressed. And you respect yourself. Mom says she has more confidence when she dresses up, and Gary told me that the salesman in his computer store who makes the most sales has a camel's hair jacket."

"Oh God!" Cass said. "I guess I'm really home."

It was wonderful having her back. The whole house sprang to life, with the phone ringing all the time, Cass running up and down the stairs, laughing, talking, telling stories about school. She was doing very well in her schoolwork but was also deeply involved in outside activities. We all wanted to be with her as much as possible. Mom took some extra days off from work and cooked and baked all sorts of foods that Cass gobbled down greedily.

"This sure beats cafeteria food," she said. "But I'll weigh a ton by the time I leave."

Gary came over the first night she was back. They spent an hour or so talking in her room, but then he left. "She's tired," he told me. "She's still on Eastern time, and she wants to get to bed early tonight. Tomorrow we'll get together again."

But Cass stayed up late talking to me. She let me come into her room, all comfortably messed up again, and we talked until after two in the morning. She was high on school, high on the East, high on her plans for the future.

"A lot of kids spend a year abroad in their junior year," she said, "but I'm thinking I might go next year. I think I'd like to go to London and study at the London School of Economics. Maybe I could also wander around France and Italy in the summer."

"But, Cass," I said, "won't you come home next summer?" My voice must have sounded desperate, because she looked at me in a puzzled way. "Well, sure," she said, "I'd certainly come home at least for a week or so before I go."

"And then if you went away to Europe next year, you wouldn't be able to come home for Christmas. Oh, Cass, I'd hate it if you didn't come home for Christmas."

She began to speak quickly then. She said I could come to visit her next Christmas in England. She said I should start saving my money, and maybe she'd be able to add something to it. I could come out for three weeks. We could have a real English Christmas and then maybe wander around Italy and Spain.

"No, no," I wailed. "I don't want to wander around Italy and Spain. I want you to come home next Christmas. Don't go away, Cass. Please, Cass, come home."

"You're too dependent on me, Penny," Cass said, reaching over and taking my hand. "It's not good for you, and it's not good for me. You're putting a heavy burden on me, and you're hiding yourself in my shadow. You've got to stop it, Penny, before you forget who you are."

Then she changed the subject. She tried to talk to me about school, about my plans for the future. She asked a lot of questions, but I was upset and barely answered.

The next morning, at breakfast, Cass said she would only be able to stay a week, that she had to be back in Cambridge on the thirtieth.

"But aren't you going to spend New Year's Eve with Gary?" I asked. "He's made all sorts of plans."

"He'll have to change them," she said. "I have some plans of my own."

She was cruel to Gary that Christmas, spending as little time as possible with him. Almost every day she arranged to see people she hardly ever bothered with before she went away to school. Gary did stay with us on Christmas day, and she oohed and ahhed over his ring and said it was "sweet." She gave him a Harvard sweatshirt and a belt she must have picked up from one of the street artists at Ghirardelli Square. She said she liked the bathrobe I made her, but when she left, I found it hanging in her closet.

Gary and I drove her to the airport on the thirtieth. He wanted to take her by himself, but she insisted that I come along. She chattered away, hardly looking at his long, melancholy face. She told me she hoped I could come East to visit her in the spring when Dad's conference would be held, but she didn't invite Gary.

When it was time for her to board her plane, she kissed him quickly, struggling out of his arms. Then she grabbed me and kissed me hard a couple of times.

"Penny," she said, "I know you're going to be fine. Just believe in yourself."

I started crying. "Please come back, Cass. Come back."

"I will. I will." She kissed me a couple more times and then ran away up the ramp.

I was crying so hard, Gary put his arms around me and pressed my head into his chest, patted my back and made soothing sounds.

"She's never coming back," I wept.

"Yes. Yes. She will. Don't cry, Penny. It will be all right. Just be patient."

And then I was laughing. When he said I should be patient, it sounded like me telling him to be patient. I started laughing, and I looked up into his sad face, and soon he smiled too. He didn't laugh, but he smiled, and he kept an arm around my shoulder as we walked back to the car.

He told me Cass had broken off with him for good. She said she would always care for him, always be his friend, and would always want to be in touch with him. But this time—and she really meant it, she said—for his good as well as hers—the break must be considered final. She told him she knew that she was a stone around his neck, preventing him from getting on with his own life and that there never could be—that there never really was—a possibility that she would ever marry him.

More than that, she told him about Decker, and about some other men she had met at Harvard. She told him things he didn't want to hear, but she told him anyway.

"And what did you say?" I asked him.

"Me?" He took a deep breath. "I said what I always say. I told her I loved her. That I would always love her and . . ."

"And?"

"And that I would be patient."

This time I didn't laugh. I just said to him, "Gary, I think the post-Christmas sales are starting at Britex next week. Come in and choose the fabric you want, and we'll start in on your jacket."

11

February was the worst month in my life. I quit my job at Britex. Not because I didn't love to work there, but because of Roseanne. I couldn't stand looking at her anymore—at her sly, scheming face and at the sharp teeth inside her smiling mouth.

I wrote a couple of hysterical letters to Cass, who didn't bother to answer. Then I tried calling her a couple of times, but she was never in. Finally, a letter came.

Darling Penny,

Stop! Stop! I told you I was finished with Gary, and you are just going to have to believe me. I don't care if he is going out with Roseanne. I'm sorry for him if he is, and I deplore his taste, but I couldn't care less. After I finish writing to you, I plan to write and tell him, "My blessings on your head, child!" Of course, it is sort of an insult to me. You would think, after all those years mooning over me, he would have been able to find somebody a little classier. But, as I've told you before, Gary's mental equipment is not up to his other charms.

I worry more about you. Why are you carrying on so? I don't want Gary, and I'm not even the slightest bit disturbed that he's going around with somebody else. In fact, I'm happy he is. I want Gary to be happy. Impossible, of course, that he should be as happy as I am. My taste is so much better.

And stop brooding about Decker! He's ancient history by

now. Not enough upstairs to keep me interested, and defi-cient in other ways that need not be itemized. But my social philosophy teacher—youngish, baldish, and very brilliant—there is a different story. Oh, Penny, he must be about the most brilliant man I've ever met. So far it's nothing much. Some long conversations in his office, one long lunch and one very long dinner. He's divorced and says he never wants any more deep commitments. But he can't keep his eyes off me in class, and I love him so much I don't think I ever knew what the word meant before.

But you! I worry about those panicky letters you wrote me. Stop living my life or Gary's life. Get on with your own. Break that ugly little sewing machine of yours and come out into the real world.

Maybe I'll give you a ring this weekend. There's a lot more I want to say to you, but my Nuclear Freeze group is meet-ing in about twenty minutes, so I've got to run.

Be happy! I am.

Love,
Cass

P.S. Don't tell Mom and Dad about my teacher.

She never did call me that weekend. I was home both days, waiting. Gary called. He wanted to tell me that the jacket I had made for him after Christmas was a real winner—that he'd been improving in his sales and that he was sure it had given him the assurance he needed.

"I wear it all the time." he said. "I practically sleep in it. As a matter of fact, I even tore the lining on the left armhole, I wear it so much."

"Bring it over," I said. "I'll fix it for you."

"Oh, it's okay," he said quickly. "It's . . . uh . . . somebody else fixed it for me."

"Oh!" I knew it must have been Roseanne, and my hatred for her surged all the way up to the roots of my hair and all the way down to the tips of my toes.

Gary cleared his throat. "Is something wrong, Penny?"

"Yes! Everything is wrong."

"Roseanne told me you quit your job at Britex."

"Yes. I quit."

"How come you didn't tell me?"

"Why should I tell you?" I cried. "I never see you anymore."

"Look, Penny, I know you're upset because I'm seeing Roseanne."

I didn't say anything.

"But, Penny, you know I've been patient. You know it's no use. She means it this time."

"No, she doesn't mean it." I could hear my voice breaking. "She always says it, but she always comes back to you. You know that, Gary."

"Penny," he said, "if I really believed it, I would wait. You know how I feel about Cass. I'll always love Cass, whatever happens. But this time it's different. And I can't sit around waiting for her. She's not sitting around waiting for me, is she?"

"I hate her!" I cried.

"Who? Cass?"

"No. Roseanne. She knew you were Cass's boyfriend. She knew it. But she went after you anyway. She didn't tell me. She acted like she was going out with some guy named Ernie, but all the time, behind my back, she was going after you."

"Cass doesn't own me, Penny," Gary said. "I don't belong to her—not anymore. She's lucky to have you for a sister. You have even more patience than I do. But you'd better give up as far as I'm concerned. She's through with me, and I need to get on with my own life."

I told Mom about Roseanne's betrayal, but she didn't see it my way at all.

"I think you're making a big fuss over nothing. Roseanne is a very nice girl. That mauve silk she saved for me last week is really a beautiful piece of material. And you know, Penny, Cass is the one who broke up with Gary. Not the other way around. Why shouldn't he go out with Roseanne?"

"Because she's a sneak and a liar. She never told me she was going after him."

"Why should she, the way you act? And you're cutting off your nose to spite your face. Why in the world did you quit your job at Britex? Now we'll never get the buys on fabrics like we used to when you worked there. Unless Roseanne puts things away for us."

Mom was working full time now for the travel agency. She had bought me a new sewing machine for Christmas, with fancy attachments. Now I could do buttonholes, hems, embroidery monograms and fancy appliqués. And she was hungry for clothes. I couldn't sew fast enough for her. There were meetings and parties that she went to after work. Soon, she said, there might be trips she could go on, free, as a representative of her agency. And in a year, she would be able to fly at very special rates all over the country and even the world.

"Maybe I'll go to Alaska next year for my vacation, or maybe even Hawaii."

"Dad never wants to go anywhere."

Mom ran her fingers through her hair. It was frosted now, and she wore it flipped over one side of her forehead. "I know," she said, "but that's his hang-up, not mine. I'll go myself, or maybe Marcia Storey would go with me. She was saying the other day that she thought I'd be a good person to travel with."

"Who's Marcia Storey?"

"That's Gina's sister. Didn't I tell you about her? Well, I met her at that cocktail party Gina threw at Christmas. Gina? Oh, that's the woman who does our visas. Anyway, Gina's sister, Marcia, is a photographer. She and I have been getting together for lunch, and once in a while we've gone to a concert. I'm sure I told you about her. She's divorced, and she knows a lot of people."

Mom didn't spend much time at home anymore. Neither did Dad. He was even busier than usual with his patients. Many evenings, I ate dinner by myself and then sewed.

But in February, even the sewing didn't make me feel better.

"I don't feel good," I told Dad one evening when he arrived home before Mom.

He blinked at me and said nervously, "Did you tell your mother?"

"She's not home yet. I'm not sick or anything. I'm just miserable. I'm so miserable, I think I want to die."

"Well," he said, "well . . ."

"Can't you do something?" I asked him. "You're supposed to do something for people who are miserable."

My father talked to me for a long time. He told me that teenagers often go through all sorts of hormonal changes which trigger emotional ups and downs. Very natural, he said, even in a stable, solid person like myself, and perhaps I should go talk to a professional psychologist who could help me see my problems a little more clearly.

"I see them pretty clearly," I said. "I don't want to go to a counselor. I'm lonely. I have no friends. Even Catherine isn't interested in me anymore. I hate school, and I'm failing geometry and English. I miss Cass, and Gary is going around with Roseanne. That's why I'm miserable."

My father waited up until my mother came home. Then the two of them went into their bedroom and fought. They fought over the next two days, both in their bedroom and in the dining room. As usual, it didn't matter if I was there or not, even if the arguments had to do with me and who was to blame because I was depressed.

For a while, Mom stayed home evenings, and Dad said I should plan to go East with him when he went in March. Mom wouldn't be able to get away from her job, but Dad said he'd like me to come if I didn't think I would miss too much school.

I assured him I would not, and the thought of seeing Cass in March made me feel better. Dad would be busy at his conference, I knew, but I would be able to spend as much time as possible with Cass. I could go with her to her classes, maybe sleep in her dorm, eat in the school cafeteria with her, talk with her, let her bully me and laugh at me and make me feel less empty.

Before we left in March, my school counselor, Ms. Dworkin, called me in to her office. "You're wasting your time, Pam," she said.

102

"Penny," I told her. "My name is Penny, not Pam."

"Yes," she said. "Penny, you're wasting your time. According to your geometry, English and civics teachers, you never hand in your work, and you're failing."

"I know," I said.

"Are you planning to go to college?" Ms. Dworkin flipped through a bunch of papers on her desk.

"No."

"Well," she said, running her eyes up and down a paper with lots of figures on it, "you have the potential, I see that, even though you apparently have never worked up to it."

"I hate school," I told her. "I'm bored all the time. There's nothing that interests me."

"Nothing?" she said. "Not even extracurricular activities? Do you belong to anything after school—chorus, drama, tennis?"

"Nothing. I hate it all. I can't wait until I graduate."

"The way you're going," Ms. Dworkin said, "you're not going to graduate."

That's when the idea of dropping out of school first came to me. Why not? I was failing in so many courses anyway. Why not drop out of school? School made me feel like I was nothing. Why should I go on feeling like that? I wasn't like Cass. I'd never be like Cass. Hadn't I always known it?

But I didn't say anything to my parents. Maybe I thought Cass would change my mind. That she would make me change my mind.

But she didn't.

We arrived in Boston on a Friday afternoon early in March. Dad's conference began the next day and ended on Tuesday afternoon. We weren't leaving until Wednesday, which should have given me plenty of time to spend with Cass.

Cass met us at our hotel that evening, and the three of us had dinner together. My father hung on everything she said, and she had a great deal to say. I felt warm and happy sitting next to her, looking at her, listening to her. She looked wonderful. Her short hair curled beautifully around her head, and her whole face looked as if she had lights inside her. She glittered and sparkled as she spoke. You could feel that her whole life was one big, glorious adventure.

"Are you still thinking of becoming a lawyer?" Dad asked.

"I don't know," Cass said. "In a way, law is too confining for me. There are so many other things I want to know about. I don't think I should lock myself into anything yet."

"That's right," Dad said, approving. "Take your time, Cass. Don't hurry."

Later, Dad said he had some people he wanted to see, so Cass and I went back to the hotel room to talk.

"Gary is still going out with Roseanne," I told her.

She waved her hand as if she were brushing off a pesty fly. "Oh, Penny, life is so marvelous for me. Simon is meeting me later, and we're driving out to a little country place he has."

"Simon?"

"My teacher. I wrote to you about him. He loves me, and oh Penny, he's great in every way. He has the weekend free, but I told him you and Dad were going to be in and I needed to be back Sunday."

"Sunday? I thought you and I . . . ."

"You and Dad have to see the sights in Boston," Cass said brightly. "I've already seen them, but you don't want to miss Paul Revere's house and the Old North Church or the Public Gardens. That's right. You can go to the Public Gardens and ride around in the famous swan boats. You and Dad will love it. Why don't you do that tomorrow, and Sunday we'll do something else. But Penny, don't say anything to Dad about Simon."

"How old is he?"

"I don't know. No more than forty, I'm sure."

"Forty!"

"I like older men," Cass said. "I guess I'm just too mature for men my own age."

"You said he was divorced."

"So what? Nowadays everybody's divorced."

I didn't answer her, and I struggled to bury my disappointment. After all, Cass was right. We should go see the sights of Boston. How many times would we be coming here, and it wasn't fair to expect her to show us around if she'd already seen everything.

Cass said she would meet us at the hotel on Sunday at about eleven for brunch, and then we would make some plans for the rest of the day. Dad had a meeting on Saturday afternoon, but he and I trudged around Boston in the morning, visiting as many sights as we could squeeze into three hours.

At eleven thirty Sunday morning, Cass called, sounding out of breath. "Listen, Penny, I'm afraid I've been delayed, so let's make it for dinner. Okay? Why don't you and Dad go see the sights today."

"We saw them yesterday, Cass, and Dad is tied up all day today."

"Well, go yourself then. You don't want to miss the

Museum of Fine Arts. I'll meet you about seven in the hotel lobby. And Penny, don't tell Dad where I am. Tell him I'm finishing a paper."

"She's finishing a paper," I told Dad. "But she says she'll meet us in the lobby at seven and that we should see some more sights."

"Well, you know I can't," Dad said. "I have a meeting at one, and then there's a speaker at four I want to hear. So why don't you go see the sights again? I think there's another sightseeing tour going to Lexington and Concord."

I wasn't interested in Lexington and Concord, just as I hadn't really been interested in Paul Revere's house or the Public Gardens. The day was cold and rainy, so I stayed in the hotel room watching TV and trying not to let a feeling of panic overpower me. I kept telling myself that Cass had a right to do what she liked, and that one of the reasons I admired her so much was that she always lived life the way she wanted, not as other people thought she should. I knew she loved me, and I knew it was all going to work out fine, I told myself. Cass would probably let me go back with her that night and spend the day with her at school. Maybe I would even meet Simon. I knew he couldn't compare to Gary, but I would try not to hate him. I would try to see him with Cass's eyes. But even if I didn't see him, I would see her room, meet her roommate and walk with her on Harvard's famous campus under the big, old trees.

Cass came running into the lobby at seven thirty. Dad and I were dressed to go out to dinner, but Cass was wearing old jeans and a rumpled jacket. She looked rumpled too, but full of even brighter lights than on Friday.

We had dinner in the hotel coffee shop. Cass ate as if she hadn't eaten the whole weekend. And she talked and laughed and asked us lots of questions, but I could see that her mind was elsewhere, and she was not listening to our answers.

"I've got to run," she said finally. "A . . . a friend is picking me up outside the hotel in ten minutes."

"Cass," I pleaded, "can I come with you? Can I stay with you for the next couple of days? It's okay with Dad. He'll be busy until Tuesday afternoon. He could meet us for dinner Tuesday night. Right, Dad?"

"Yes," Dad said. "Penny's been looking forward to being with you, Cass."

"I can get my bag, Cass. I'm all packed. It will only take a few minutes."

She was looking at me. Her eyes moved up and down the new brown herringbone wool suit I had made for this trip with the coordinating beige silk blouse. They settled on my shoes and matching purse, but not on my face, as she said, "I'm sorry, Penny. I . . . it's going to be a very busy day for me tomorrow. I need to finish one paper and study for an exam on Tuesday morning, but maybe Tuesday afternoon . . ."

She was ashamed of me. She didn't want Simon to see me. She didn't want me to come back with her because she was ashamed of me. But why? My suit was one I had seen featured in *Harper's Bazaar,* and the shoes and purse were expensive Italian ones that I'd bought half-price on sale at I. Magnin's.

My hands began shaking. I must have knocked my purse off the table as I stood up and yelled at her, "No. I don't want to see you on Tuesday. I won't be here on Tuesday. I'm going home tomorrow. I'm sorry I came.

I hate you, Cass, and I'm dropping out of school. You wouldn't want your friends to meet me. Not your roommate. Not your divorced, middle-aged boyfriend. You wouldn't want them to know your sister is a high-school dropout."

12

Dad tried to patch it up. He got Cass to say I could come back with her. He told her, in front of me, that I had been depressed and had looked forward to being with her.

"She knew that," I shouted. "I wrote her I was depressed. I told her I needed to see her and talk to her. I wrote her all that, but she's so busy fooling around with her creepy teacher, she doesn't care anything about me."

Dad said of course she did. Cass said of course she did. But I went home the next day, and a week later I took the high school equivalency test.

Suddenly I felt good. And bad. Good because I was doing what I wanted to do. What I knew was best for me. And bad because I was so angry at Cass I hated her. And I had never hated Cass before.

Cass called me every day for about a week. After that, her calls tapered off, but not the urgency in her voice.

"You can't drop out of school, Penny. You're only doing it to spite me. You're ruining your life just to spite me."

"No," I told her. "I want to get on with my life. Isn't that what you always told me to do? And that's why I took the equivalency test. I know I passed it—it was a snap."

"Because you're bright," Cass yelled. "You could be a real winner if you only tried."

"I'll be a real winner in my own way, Cass. I'm sick of trying to please you. I'm finished with that."

"Listen, Penny, listen! I know I was horrible. I know I failed you when you needed me. But, Penny, I really do love you very much. You know that, don't you?"

"No," I said. "I don't."

"Look, Penny, I was a selfish pig, okay? I didn't think of you. But I'm human. I make mistakes. I'll try not to let it happen again."

"You were ashamed of me."

"No, no."

"Oh, yes. You were ashamed of me. You'll always be ashamed of me."

"I love you, Penny, and I don't want you to ruin your life."

"I'm dropping out of school, Cass. As soon as I hear I passed, I'm dropping out."

I got a job in a bridal shop in Stonestown. The boss, Renee Limon, was looking for somebody full time, but I told her I'd be finished with school in about six weeks—once my scores came through—and then I could work full time. Most of the dresses in the shop were ready-made and only needed alterations. But if a customer insisted and was willing to pay, Renee said, the shop could make the clothes of the whole wedding party.

She liked my work, but Alexis and Florence, the two other seamstresses, kept trying to put me down. I despised them from the start. They did sloppy work. Their seams puckered, and their darts never really lay flat.

But I didn't say anything at first. I was happy. I couldn't wait to go to work and see the brides-to-be and their families. No place is happier than a bridal shop.

Right from the start, I knew that the shop could be improved to give it a romantic but more classy appearance. I wanted an antique Italian look with period furniture, hand-painted wallpaper and mirrors in carved wooden frames. I began gobbling up articles in *Architectural Digest* and taking books out of the library on interior design.

At first, my parents tried to persuade me to stay in school and graduate. I didn't budge. After a while, they gave in. Mom first. She saw that I was happy, and she said maybe that was the important thing. Dad held out a little longer, but finally he agreed too. He said the son of a colleague had dropped out of high school but had returned a few years later and was currently finishing his Ph.D. in chemistry at Stanford.

Gary dropped by to see me.

"I heard from Cass," he said.

Gary was wearing the camel's hair jacket, but there were spots on his left lapel and some big specks of fluff along one sleeve. I started brushing them off.

"She wants me to talk to you," he said. "She doesn't think you should drop out of school."

"Gary," I said, "your jacket needs to be cleaned."

"Oh," he said, "I hadn't noticed. I guess I wear it too often."

"You need another one," I told him. "Or maybe you should get somebody to make you a gray blazer. A double-breasted one. I saw this guy—he's marrying one of our customers. He came into the shop yesterday while she was trying on her dress, and he was wearing a double-breasted gray flannel blazer with navy pants, a light blue shirt and a wonderful tie with pink pigs and red roses on it."

I started laughing, thinking about the tie. There was so much happiness in my job, some was always left over to rub off on me.

"Roseanne broke off with me," Gary said glumly.

"No kidding!" I wanted to jump up and down and scream hooray, but I managed to compose my face into a serious, sympathetic expression.

"She said it was obvious I didn't really have my heart in the relationship. Besides, she met somebody who she says was more fun."

"You're better off," I told him. "I tried to warn you, but you wouldn't listen."

"No, you didn't," he said. "You didn't try to warn me."

"I told you to be patient."

"No," he said. "Forget that. Cass isn't interested in me. She'll never be interested in me."

"She wrote you a letter."

"Because she wanted me to come over and talk to you about dropping out of school." His eyes focused on my face. "What's the story with you anyway?"

"I'm sick of school," I said. "You know I never liked school. There's nothing that interests me, and I'm failing everything. Why should I stay in school if I hate it so much? I'm really happy now, Gary. The last couple of months haven't been so good for me, but I'm happy now."

"Why didn't you call me?" he said. "Why didn't you tell me you were so miserable? I didn't even know."

"You were busy."

"But I'm never so busy I don't have time for you, Penny. You should know that. You were always one of my best friends. You listened to me when I was down. You always helped me feel better. I want you to think of me as your friend. I want you to know I'm here when you need me."

I promised that I would call him if I ever needed him again, and I made him promise to go and have his jacket cleaned. He forgot that he was supposed to persuade me not to drop out of school.

In April, I hardly went to school at all. Sometimes I worked extra hours in the bridal shop, and other times I began redoing the dining room.

Mom wanted to buy new furniture. "Copenhagen is having a sale," she said. "I can get a new Danish dining-room table and chairs for half-price."

"Forget it," I told her. "Our old furniture has more character."

"Character?" Mom said disdainfully. "Your father's mother passed it on to us when we got married. She didn't want it anymore—it was so old-fashioned. She bought herself a new Danish set, and we've been stuck with her old castoffs all these years. Your father was always too cheap to buy a new set, but now we can easily afford it."

"Danish is considered old-fashioned now," I told her, having just read an article in one of my magazines, "but this nice, old, heavy mahogany is in. We can polish it up, and I'll replace the cushions, maybe with a green and white striped fabric. Then we need to paint the room—I think in a soft cream color to set off the dark wood. We can put new shutters on the windows, and I'll make slim side drapes to match the cushions." I persuaded Mom to buy a crystal chandelier to hang over the table, and when the room was finished, it looked stunning.

"I love it," Mom said. "I just love it."

"I liked it better the other way," Dad said, "and it's crazy to buy such an expensive glass chandelier. What if we have an earthquake?"

"What if we have a tidal wave?" Mom countered, and they were off again.

I offered to redo the living room. By this time, I realized what an embarrassing hodgepodge it was and how much my own taste had developed. Mom refused. She said she liked it, but she did ask me to help her redecorate her bedroom.

"Marcia Storey's bedroom is painted a gray blue, and she has a shiny, quilted bedspread in bright blues and lavenders."

"Well," I said, "we'll do whatever you like, but . . ."

"The drapes pick up the lavender, and she uses colored venetian blinds, the same color as the walls. She has a chaise lounge in solid lavender velveteen and two darling little glass tables on either side of the bed."

I finally persuaded her that less was better than more, and that the minimal look was now in for bedrooms. We did the whole thing with beautiful Japanese-designed bed sheets, huge straw baskets filled with dried plants, and dramatic lighting. Over Dad's objections, we cleared away all clutter and unnecessary pieces of furniture. We also ripped up the old, faded blue carpet and refinished the floor in a dark, almost black, stain.

The bedroom took the latter part of April, and in the beginning of May I received word that I had passed the equivalency test.

"Are you sure you want to drop out?" Dad said. "You can still change your mind."

"I'd have to repeat the whole term," I told him. "No Dad, I want to quit. I'm so happy, I wish I could do something to make you happy too."

"You can," Dad said.

"What?"

"Just don't redecorate the bathroom. That's about the only place left in the house where I feel comfortable."

I felt so happy, I made up with Cass. I called her one evening and, for a change, I got her in.

"Cass, it's Penny."

"Penny! I'm so glad to hear from you. I was going to call you tomorrow—really I was."

"It's okay, Cass. I just wanted you to know I passed the equivalency test."

Silence.

"I'm really happy now, Cass. I felt like a loser in school. You'll just have to accept that. My job means a lot to me. I'm really good—better than good—and already, Cass, I've got lots of ideas to improve the shop."

"Well," Cass said slowly, "I guess there's nothing I can say that will change your mind."

"No. Nothing."

"It's just that I'd hate to feel it was because you were angry with me. I've been kicking myself because I know I failed you. I feel terrible about that."

"Cass," I told her, "I had been thinking about dropping out before I came to Boston. I didn't do it to spite you. That's why I'm calling. I don't want you to feel bad. Sure, I was angry and disappointed. But not anymore. I'm really happy now, Cass. And I wanted to tell you I was."

"Okay, Penny. I'm glad about that."

"I have some really good ideas, Cass, about the shop."

She didn't seem interested in the shop or my ideas. So we began talking about her. School would be over soon, and she and Simon were planning to leave for Europe. He wanted to take her to Normandy and Brittany, and he had some friends in Alsace. Then, in September, she would head for London and start school.

"Aren't you coming home?" I asked her.

She hesitated. "I don't know if I can, Penny. I'd like to, but I'm not sure I'll have the time."

"Oh."

"Of course, I could if you really needed me, Penny. I'm never again going to make the kind of mistake I made in March. If you ever really need me, you know I'll come."

"Gary broke up with Roseanne," I told her.

"Gary?" She sounded as if she didn't know who I was talking about.

"Gary. Gary Summers."

"Oh! Well—he'll find somebody else, I'm sure."

"You really don't care, Cass?" I could feel my ears burning, and a great balloon of happiness pressing against my chest.

"I really don't, Penny. But I do care about you. So if you need me, remember, I'm here."

"I'll remember," I said, but I knew I'd never need her help, ever again.

"And I'm glad you're not angry anymore."

"Aren't you going to wish me good luck, Cass?"

"Well, sure I am, Penny. I always wish you good luck. You know that. Whatever you do."

"Good night, Cass."

"Good night, Penny."

13

The shop was really busy in May, what with all the June weddings coming up. Some nights I worked late, and one Sunday Renee asked me to come in for a few hours, and I ended up staying the whole day.

Alexis and Florence couldn't work overtime. Both of them were married with kids, and Florence had an old, diabetic mother who lived with her and needed a lot of attention. Renee told me that Florence had once worked for a very fancy bridal shop in New York, but I didn't believe it. She was supposed to do all the difficult dresses and alterations, while Alexis and I worked on less complicated ones. It infuriated me to see how sloppy her work was, but Renee didn't seem to know the difference and most of our customers were too happy to care.

But when we did the dresses for the De Mateo wedding party, Florence's sloppiness became apparent to others besides myself. The bride, Victoria De Mateo, was a tall, slim girl who reminded me of Sophia Loren, except she had a bigger nose and a smaller bust. I really liked her—she was so happy. She couldn't stop talking about her wedding, her boyfriend, her honeymoon, her plans for the future. Her mother was almost as happy as she. Victoria was her only daughter, her youngest. Two older brothers had married girls whose parents, according to Mrs. De Mateo, had given them cheap, shabby weddings. "But for my Victoria, we're pulling out all the stops."

We were making the dresses for the whole wedding party. Victoria wanted a picture-book wedding dress with a full, swirling skirt, ribbons, ruffles, an elaborate lace bodice and lace trim on the sleeves and skirt. I loved the pattern she had selected, but Florence was to make the wedding gown while Alexis and I worked on the dresses for the bridesmaids and maid of honor.

I had to choke down my horror when I saw the way Florence was handling the imported reembroidered lace on the bodice and how the lace galloon on the chiffon skirt puckered. When she did the hem, which should have been hand-rolled, she made it too short and used a horsehair braid which cannot be lengthened. I was there when Victoria came in for the final fitting, and I watched her face in the mirror lose its smile of anticipation.

"It's just gorgeous on you," Florence cooed.

"But . . ." Victoria began.

"Gorgeous!" Renee echoed.

This time I wasn't the only one who could see every sloppy dart, every mismatched piece of lace, every pull and pucker, and the hem which was at least an inch too short.

Victoria turned to her mother with a frightened look on her face. "Mother," she said, "it's not right."

Later, when Renee and I were alone, she said, "It really is a pain doing dresses from scratch. I always prefer selling ready-mades."

"It doesn't have to be a pain," I said slowly. "Not if the work is good."

I didn't say anything more, but she asked me. "What was wrong with that dress?"

I told her what was wrong. She said that Florence had been working for her for seven years, and that she had once worked for a fancy bridal shop in New York. "Maybe she did work for a fancy bridal shop in New York," I told Renee, "but if she did, she didn't make wedding gowns."

I wasn't trying to show Florence up, as she said later, but I was, am, and always will be disgusted by shoddy work. That was why Renee asked me to come in that Sunday to repair the mess Florence had made on Victoria's gown. I couldn't do everything I would have liked to, but when Victoria tried the gown on after I had finished, I had the pleasure of seeing her face full of the smiles that should cover the face of every bride.

Other things fell into place for me in May. I was in love with all the brides and their dresses. I smiled with them as they looked at themselves in the long three-way mirrors, over the peau de soie, the satin, chiffon, crepe de chine. . . . I loved murmuring the names of the laces—Alençon, Chantilly, peau d'ange. I visited florists, familiarizing myself with every possible flower that could be included in the bridal bouquet. I learned to differentiate between a calla lily and a chrysanthemum. I sniffed freesia, carnations and sweetheart roses.

And I thought of Gary. Especially when I smelled the sweetheart roses. I remembered how Cass said she didn't really care about him, and I wondered why I had waited so long.

So I called Gary.

"Did you get your jacket cleaned?" I asked him.

"Well, yes, I did," he said. "I still keep wearing it, even though it's getting too warm. That salesman I told you about, Bill Ferguson, he's wearing a gray raw silk and cotton jacket, and he's still the best salesman in the place.'"

I didn't offer to make him a raw silk and cotton jacket, but I did tell him about my job.

"The boss really likes me," I told him, "but the other women hate me."

"How could anybody hate you?"

"Oh, they do. They're jealous. Because they know I'm so much better than they are. Renee, my boss, she knows it too, now. She's a little nervous because one of the women—Florence—has been there seven years, but lately Renee has been giving me the really difficult dresses to do. Florence waited for me outside yesterday, after work, to tell me she thought I was trying to show her up and that she knew I was trying to get her to quit."

"Have you heard from Cass?"

"Not recently. Maybe a couple of weeks ago. She's going to Europe with Simon. He's her teacher. And then she's going to London for a year. So anyway, I didn't say anything to Florence. She's not going to quit. She's got a family to support and a diabetic mother. And she's fast and okay on simple alterations. We really need to get rid of Alexis and hire someone who can do quality work like me, and maybe a couple of other top workers. Then we can expand the business and do dresses for more wedding parties. There's lots of money in that."

"Hey, Penny, is that you talking?"

"It's me, all right, Gary. I love this business. Renee is okay, but she's getting old and she doesn't have much imagination. Do you know what I'd really like?"

"What?"

"I'd like to go into partnership with her. Maybe not right away. After a year or so. I bet you we could turn that little store into the biggest and best bridal shop in San Francisco. Maybe we could even hire our own designer. . . ."

Gary started laughing. "You sound like a career woman, Penny. You don't sound like you. You sound like . . . like Cass."

"Like Cass?"

"Well, yes. Just then, when you were planning on turning that store into a million-dollar business. You sounded so confident and sure of yourself."

"But I can, Gary. I know I can."

"Well, that's just great, Penny. It's good to know you're so happy."

"I am, Gary. I'm very happy. And what about you?"

"Oh—things are okay. They like me at work, I guess. And school's okay. Everything is okay." His voice sounded flat.

"Are you going around with anybody?"

He snorted. "Now and then. Nothing that matters."

"Okay, Gary, I tell you what. Let's get together one night. How about this Saturday? Are you free? I'll take you out to dinner. I owe you one."

"Saturday's not so good. I'm supposed to go to the Russian River with Darryl on Saturday. Somebody there has a motorcycle he might want to buy. We might stay overnight. How about Friday or Sunday?"

"Oh! Well—sure, Gary. Whenever."

"You sound disappointed. Is Saturday something special?"

"No, no. Not really."

"Come on, Baby Sister. You can't fool old Gary. What is it?"

122

"Well, it's just my birthday. But that's okay. We can make it on Friday."

"No, we can't. I'll go with Darryl some other time. You're on for Saturday."

"Great. And it will be my treat."

"No, it won't."

"But I asked you first."

"But I'm bigger than you and meaner."

By the time I hung up, both of us were laughing like we used to do a couple of years ago when he hung around the house with me, waiting for Cass.

Saturday night, we sat in that restaurant talking until we were the last couple there and the waiter began rattling dishes all around us and sweeping up the floors.

"I think they're giving us a hint," Gary said, and I laughed and laughed and laughed even though it wasn't all that funny.

He drove me home and parked, but we started talking again. I can't even remember about what. We both kept talking at each other—talking and laughing—holding the other one there as if each of us knew there was something else to say and we were waiting for the other one to say it.

All of a sudden we both stopped talking at exactly the same time. I began thinking—desperately—trying to figure out how to say it. The quiet grew awful, and finally Gary said, "I guess you want to go in."

"No," I said, "I don't, but it is late, and you probably . . ."

"No," he said, and then he grinned at me. Gary has the most beautiful smile of anybody I know. "A dentist's dream," Cass used to say, because his teeth are so white and perfectly shaped. But it isn't only his teeth. When Gary smiles, his whole face smiles.

"I love you, Gary," I said. Just like that. I came right out with it, and it was so easy and natural.

"I love you too, Penny," he said, and his hand began patting my shoulder.

"No, no, Gary," I said. "Not that way. I really love you. I think you're the most wonderful guy in the world. I've always loved you, and I always will."

I grabbed him around the neck and kissed him hard on his mouth. (He was still smiling. It all happened so fast, he didn't even have a chance to close his mouth.) Then I leaped out of the car and tore off into my house.

I didn't want him to say a single thing. Not yet. I only wanted to carry the joy of the most perfect night of my life into the house with me and keep it all to myself.

14

Gary called me at nine the next morning. And I was ready.

"I didn't wake you, did I, Penny?"

"No, you didn't, Gary."

"Well, I've been awake a long time. I've been thinking. Penny, I . . ."

"Look, Gary," I said, "why don't you come right over? I'll be waiting for you outside. We can go for a walk on the beach. We'll talk."

The day was so warm and golden, I left my shoes in the car and walked barefoot on the wet sand along the ocean's edge. Gary kept his shoes on. He didn't look at me at first, and he walked so fast I had to run to keep up with him.

"Slow down," I told him. "I can't keep up with you."

He slowed down and began talking, his eyes down on the ground. "Penny, I don't know . . . Last night . . . I guess I must have had a little too much to drink. I'm sorry because I'm not sure . . ."

"I'm sure," I told him. "You didn't do anything. I was the one who told you I loved you, and I do, Gary, I do. I always have. I always will."

"But . . ." He stopped, hesitated and looked at me with a long, sad face.

"No buts, Gary." I reached out and took his hand.

"You love me too. I know you do. You said you did last night."

"I do," Gary said, "but I don't know if I love you that way."

"Yes, you do, Gary. You really do. I know you think you love Cass too."

Gary didn't answer.

"Well, it's all right if you think you do. I love her too. But you and I—we're different from Cass. We want a kind of life that's not the kind of life she wants."

"I know that," Gary said.

We were standing there by the water's edge, holding hands. Actually, I was holding his hand, but he wasn't holding mine. He was simply letting me hold his. It didn't worry me or frighten me. I saw the sunlight leaping on the waves and I pressed his hand. "We've always been happy when we're together, Gary."

"Yes, that's true. But . . ."

"You're just not used to thinking of me as anything but Cass's baby sister. Look at me, Gary. I'm grown-up now. I'm seventeen and I'm grown-up."

He looked, and I could feel his hand slowly tightening inside of my own. "But you've never gone out with anybody else," he said. "You're just a kid. You don't know what you're saying."

"I do know. I do," I told him. "I don't need to go out with anybody else because it's always been you. I didn't know it. I thought I wanted you and Cass to end up together. But now I know it's always been you. You were always my idol."

"I didn't know that."

"I always thought you were the greatest-looking guy I ever saw. But it wasn't only what you looked like. Cass loved the way you looked too. I guess lots of girls did.

126

But to me it really wasn't important what you looked like on the outside. It was what you were—deep inside. You were special. There was never anybody like you."

"I'm ordinary," he said shyly, looking at me as if he were meeting me for the first time.

"No," I yelled, "you're not ordinary. You're wonderful. You're the most wonderful, sensitive person in the whole world. There's nobody like you."

Gary shook his head, but the color rose up in his face.

"Listen to me, Gary," I told him. "Do you remember that time on the library steps, when Cass was doing some research on something or other? And you and I sat there, waiting for her? Do you remember?"

"Yes," Gary said, "I do remember. I held your hand, and those two girls came up the stairs, and they giggled. . . ."

"Yes, yes. That's exactly what happened."

"And you dropped my hand."

"No," I cried. "You dropped my hand, because I remember how disappointed I felt. I think it was then I began to understand how I felt about you."

"You dropped my hand," Gary insisted. "I know because lately, whenever I think about Cass, I keep remembering how you and I sat there planning for the senior prom and how you dropped my hand. Maybe if you hadn't . . ."

We stopped walking and stood on the warm, wet sand, looking at each other.

"You were always good to me," Gary murmured. He was holding my hand now as hard as I was holding his. "But I thought it was because she was your sister."

"I thought so, too." I laughed out loud. "But Gary,

it was because I loved you. Because I always loved you."

And then he picked me up and held me tight against him. I hung there laughing, my feet dangling off the ground, and this time he was kissing me and murmuring, "I didn't know. I didn't know."

Later, we must have walked for miles and miles along the beach, holding hands, talking, laughing, and every so often, stopping to kiss. Gary couldn't stop talking. He told me maybe he had always loved me—or maybe it was the kind of person I was—the kind of person he thought or hoped Cass might become. He had to do some more thinking about it, he said, but maybe what he had felt for Cass wasn't really love. Maybe it was just kind of a wild infatuation with some impossible dream.

"Yes, yes," I said. "It was impossible. It was always impossible."

"But you kept telling me to be patient. You always told me to be patient."

"Maybe because I didn't want to lose you. I didn't know then that was the reason, but that must have been it. I must have always known it would never work out for you and Cass."

"Maybe it was you I always really loved," he said. "All those times you spent comforting me and listening to me while Cass was off somewhere doing her own thing. I was always happiest when I was with you." He hit his head with his free hand. "What a jerk I've been!"

"We've both been jerks," I told him. "But I guess I did know ahead of you that we were right for each other."

"I would have figured it out," Gary said. "Everything's been so blah lately. I thought it was because of

128

Cass, but now I know it's because I wasn't seeing you anymore. I didn't have anybody to talk to. Roseanne was a real drag. I would have figured it out, Penny. I know I would have."

We walked all the way to Fort Funston, and then we sat on the warm sand and talked some more.

"What do you think Cass will say?" Gary asked, running his fingers through the sand.

"It won't matter to her," I told him. And I really believed it.

"I want her to be happy too," Gary said. "I worry about her."

"You don't have to worry about Cass. She'll be fine. She'll go from man to man, but she won't make any of them happy."

Gary was shocked. "How can you say such a thing, Penny? You always stuck up for her."

"I love Cass," I said. "I'll always love her, but I wouldn't want anybody I cared about to be involved with her. She doesn't care about anybody but herself."

"She cares about you."

"No, she doesn't. Only herself."

I phoned home to tell whoever was there that I would be spending the day with Gary. Mom answered the phone, sounding breathless.

"Hi, Mom."

"Oh, it's you, Penny? I was on my way out when I heard the phone ring. I was meeting Marcia for lunch, and I left you a note telling you I wouldn't be back until later."

"I'm going to be spending the day with Gary, Mom. We might pick up some food for dinner later and cook at home."

"Don't expect me for dinner. I might go to a movie

with Marcia and eat out with her later. I don't remember where Dad said he was going. I know he has patients this morning, but I think he said he might be having dinner with his sister. Anyway, I have to run now."

"Mom, Gary and I are in love."

"What?"

"We're in love."

"My God!" Mom said. "I've got to run, but what will Cass say?"

Dad didn't seem worried when he heard. "Well," he said, "well—Gary's a nice boy. I always thought he was a nice boy."

"You didn't think he was such a nice boy when Cass was going out with him," Mom snapped.

"It's okay, Mom," I said. "It's okay."

"No," Dad said slowly, chewing on a piece of English muffin. It was early the next day, and we were all having breakfast together before leaving for work. "I never said he wasn't a nice boy. I always thought he was a nice boy, but . . ."

"But not good enough for your precious Cass. Good enough for Penny, but not Cass," Mom yelled, pushing away her bowl of granola.

"But he's right, Mom."

She kept glaring at Dad, not hearing me, as usual, whenever she and Dad fought. She was preparing to really tell him off, but I tapped her on the arm and said "MOM!" in a loud voice. She turned and looked at me, surprised.

"Listen to me, Mom—Dad is right. Gary wasn't for Cass. But he is for me. He likes the same things I like. He wants the same things out of life I want. We're perfect together."

"He's only your first," Mom said. "Wait until you've dated other boys."

"I don't want to date other boys."

"You're only seventeen," Mom said desperately. "Don't lock yourself in. Don't . . ." She looked at Dad, and I knew what she was thinking. Don't end up with the first boy you go out with. Don't end up before you begin.

Dad took a deep breath. "Your mother's right, Penny. Take your time. You're young. You don't know what you want yet. Don't hurry."

But I knew what I wanted. In the next couple of weeks, Gary and I saw each other at least once every day, and we talked about what we wanted. His ideas weren't as definite as mine. He thought computers were the way he would go, and as for me—all he could say was that he felt so happy and calm—he didn't think he had ever felt that way in his whole life.

I told him what I wanted. "I want to make that shop into the biggest and best bridal shop in San Francisco. Maybe in the Bay Area. I need to learn a lot—not so much about sewing, but about business. Maybe I should go with you to City College at night and take some business administration courses. I need to understand how a successful business operates and how to advertise and bring in customers. Yesterday we got a whole new order from a girl who's getting married in September. She's a friend of Victoria De Mateo—Wendy Cooper—a cute little blonde girl. Maybe a little dumpy, but she hopes to lose ten pounds, and I told her we don't have to do the final fitting until August. I'm doing her dress, a real beauty in ivory silk organza over satin. It has a dropped waist, high neck and gathered back with bishop sleeves. And I guess I'll do her mother's dress too. Anyway, she was recommended to me personally. Victoria told her not to let anybody else make her dress, and she told me that one of her friends is planning a December wedding. Renee just gave me a raise. I bet you, in another year I'll be bringing her more business than she ever thought possible. Then I'll talk to her about a partnership."

"And me?" Gary asked. "What about me?"

I was sitting on his lap, curled up against his chest, and I looked at him, startled.

"You?"

"Yes," he said. "Sometimes you sound like Cass. Sometimes it sounds as if there's no place for me in your plans."

"No," I said, my arms around his neck now. "I'm not like Cass. Don't say that. I never make any plans without you. I want to be with you all my life. I never want to be away from you. I want to marry you, Gary."

"We're too young to get married," Gary said slowly, but I could tell he liked the idea. I think I know Gary better than he knows himself.

"You'll be twenty in November, and I'll be eighteen next May. We could get married on my birthday," I told him.

"Do you really want to marry me?" Gary asked in a shaky voice.

"The trouble with you, Gary," I told him, "is that you have no confidence. Cass used to say she was bad for you, and she was. The only good thing about you and Cass is that you met me. You're never going to feel unsure about me. I love you. I want to marry you. I'll always want to marry you, so the rest is up to you."

"I think I want to marry you too."

132

"You don't have to make up your mind now, Gary. I'll wait for you. You're the only one I want. But if you need to take your time . . ."

"No!" Gary said. "I'm sick of playing the field. You're right. We're both young, but we're not like Cass. We don't want to be hopping from one love affair to another. I don't want it. I want to be happy with one person. I want to feel there's one person who loves me best in the world and who I love best."

"That's me," I said, bending his head down and kissing his big, spreading cowlick.

After that, Gary and I spent all our free time together.

"When are you going to tell Cass?" Gary kept asking.

I knew he was frightened, and so was I. I kept putting it off. I needed a little more time to build up my courage. Finally, a week or so before she was ready to leave for France, I told him I thought I would write her a letter.

"Maybe you should wait until the end of summer," Gary said.

"Why? Nothing's going to change, will it?"

"No, no!" Gary picked me up and pressed me against him. He picks me up a lot and carries me around. I'm so small and thin compared to Cass. He never could pick her up and carry her around the way he can with me.

"So why shouldn't I tell her now?"

His face was buried in my hair. "Your hair smells so clean," he said. "Cass's hair always smelled like . . . like . . ."

"Like a barnyard," I told him. "Because she hardly

ever remembers to wash her hair. She's such a slob."

Both of us laughed uneasily.

"So, I'm going to tell her. Okay?"

"I guess so, Penny," Gary said. "If you think it's the right time."

"It's the right time," I told him.

15

Cass came home.

First she screamed at me over the phone, and then two days later she came home.

She was waiting for me when I stepped through the door, after work. Mom and Dad were with her in the dining room, and she leaped up at me as I came into the room.

"Hi, Cass," I said, smiling, coming toward her with my arms out.

I could see she'd been crying. Her face was red and swollen. When I kissed her, I could smell her unwashed hair. She pulled away from me and grabbed my shoulders.

"Penny," she said, "I think you're crazy."

"No," I said. "I'm not crazy."

"Yes, you are. You are. I always knew something was wrong with you, but I didn't realize how sick you really are. You need help, Penny. Right away."

I sat down, smoothing the new dove-colored linen dress that I had run up as soon as I heard Cass was coming home. I set my purse down and looked at her standing there with her disheveled hair, her red, puffy face and her wrinkled clothes. Stay calm, I told myself. Speak slowly. I had been practicing, in front of the mirror, staying calm before Cass.

"I'm not crazy," I said carefully. "I'm very happy, Cass, and I think if anybody needs help it must be you."

"Why don't we have dinner," Mom said. "Let's get something to eat, and then we can talk."

"That's right," Dad said, jumping up. "Come on, Linda, I'll give you a hand."

"I'm not hungry." Cass sounded like a sulky little child.

"You'll feel better after you eat," Mom said, putting an arm around Cass's shoulder.

She shook Mom off. "How could you let her do it?" she demanded.

"Well, really, Cass," Mom said, "it didn't have anything to do with me. As a matter of fact, I told her not to get seriously involved with Gary. After all, he's only the first boy she's ever gone out with. I did tell her, didn't I, Penny?"

"I did too," Dad said. "She's too young to lock herself into a permanent relationship."

"Permanent?" Cass yelled.

"Yes, permanent," I said in a shaky voice. "I'm going to marry Gary. On my birthday. When I'm eighteen."

Everybody started yelling then. I had to struggle to keep down the panic that was rising inside me.

Finally, as steadily as I could, I said to Cass right in the middle of a hysterical outburst, "You don't want Gary. So why should you care if I do?"

She put her hands out toward me and said, pleading, "Because he's not right for you, Penny. Can't you see that? You're going to get hurt. That's why I care."

"No," I said. "That's not true. I'm not going to get hurt, and you know it. You don't care about me. You don't care about anybody but yourself."

136

Suddenly I was crying, and Cass knelt down beside me and gathered me up in her arms. "I do care about you," she crooned, rocking me like she used to. "I love you, Penny. You know that. I know you've been lonely. I know you've missed me. I've missed you too. But maybe we can change all that."

She kissed the top of my head. "At Christmas, you can come to England and . . ."

Cass's arms were warm but I pulled away from her and looked at her beautiful face full of love. "No," I said, "I can't come to England at Christmas, because I'll be busy working on my wedding dress."

The love faded. "You're only doing this to spite me," Cass said.

"No, Cass, that's not so. I love Gary. I've always loved Gary."

"You're doing it to spite me," she said, her eyes narrowing. "You're getting back at me because you can't have me here whenever you need to have your nose wiped. You never were able to live your own life. You always had to try to live mine. You spied on me and read my diary. You never let me be."

"You never let *me* be," I cried. "You always tried to make me into you. You never let me be myself."

"Girls! Girls!" Mom said.

"And now you have to take Gary," Cass yelled. "Because you know he's a part of my life. You've got to steal something that belongs to me."

"No! No! No!" I pleaded. "He doesn't belong to you. He never belonged to you. And you didn't want him. You said you didn't want him. He doesn't belong to you. He belongs to me."

"It's a power trip," Cass screamed, one finger pointing at me. "That's all it is." She looked wildly around the room. "Just look at this place—it's like a funeral parlor. I don't recognize any room in this house anymore."

"The bathroom is the same," Dad said. "I made her promise not to change the bathroom."

"It's like you're the only one who lives here now. Like you've destroyed everybody else's traces. I don't even feel like this is my home."

"Your room's the same," Mom said. "And I must say, Cass, I was delighted with the way Penny redid the dining room and my bedroom. I agreed with everything she did. And we'll probably redo the living room again too."

"You want to be me," Cass cried. "You always wanted to be me."

"I don't want to be you," I said. "I'm happy now because I'm me. You would never let me be me. You were never interested in the real me. I'm good, but you don't even know or care how good I am or what I want to do with my life."

I stopped because I could see she wasn't listening. She would never listen.

"Gary doesn't love you," Cass said. Now she was cool and calm.

"He does. He does."

"He's marrying you on the rebound. He doesn't love you."

"No! No! He loves me." I could feel my knees trembling.

"He'll never love you, and you'll always know it if you marry him."

Mom said carefully, "I really don't think that's true, Cass. Gary does seem very fond of Penny, and I don't

138

understand why you're making such a fuss. After all, you did break off with him, didn't you? And you're not really interested in him anymore, are you?"

Cass stood there, not answering.

I waited, feeling the terror mount inside me.

"Are you?"

"No," she said finally. "I'm not interested in him."

"So?" Mom said gently. "I don't think Penny should get married. Not yet, anyway. But I really can't see anything wrong with her going around with Gary. He is a nice boy. I always thought he was a nice boy, even when . . . even when you were going around with him."

"He's a birdbrain," Cass said.

"Maybe you think he is," I shrieked. "You always made him feel inadequate. But I love him, and I think he's wonderful."

"Mr. and Mrs. America," Cass taunted.

She only stayed three days. Over and over again, she talked to me. She yelled at me and pleaded with me. She told me not to marry Gary, not to marry young like Mom. I'd regret it if I did, just as Mom regretted it. No, I told her, I would not regret it, because I knew what I was going to do with my life, even when I was married. I tried to tell her how serious I felt about my work, but she kept saying over and over again, "You're just like Mom. All you ever want is fun." She didn't hear anything I said, and finally I just stopped trying.

But I was afraid. I knew she was going to see Gary alone, even if she didn't tell me so herself.

"She's meeting me after work," Gary said over the phone. I had asked him not to come to the house while she was there.

"You don't have to meet her," I told him. "You can just say no."

"I can't do that, Penny."

"Why not?"

"Well—because . . ."

"You don't have any backbone when it comes to Cass," I said nervously. "She turns you into a jellyfish."

"No, no," he said. "It's just that we did have a—a relationship for a long time. I can't say no after all those years."

"She said no to you, Gary. Remember that. She doesn't care about you. She never did. I used to read her diary. I never told you that, but I did. She was always using you. Don't be a fool, Gary. Say no."

"I love you, Penny. It's not going to matter if I meet Cass. You'll see."

That day, I was so frightened, I couldn't even sew a straight seam. I kept snarling up the thread in the machine, and I could see Florence watching me with a malicious smile. Mom and Dad had dinner with me that night, but none of us said anything about Cass and Gary. Dad talked about politics, and Mom tried to get me interested in the fall fashions. She wanted to know if I really thought the color green was on its way back in again.

My hands shook all through the evening. I couldn't do anything. I couldn't sew or watch television or iron a new red Marimekko dress I had finished over the last weekend. I was going to wear it to a picnic Gary's company was having on the Fourth of July.

My hands kept shaking. I took a long, hot shower and tried to calm down.

"I'm scared," I told Mom, coming down the stairs and showing her how my hands were shaking. "If Gary breaks up with me, I don't want to live."

Mom gave me a sleeping pill and came upstairs to sit on my bed.

"It's going to be all right," she said. "I know it will all turn out for the best."

I fell asleep, and when I woke up dawn was breaking. I leaped up out of bed and hurried to Cass's bedroom. Her door was closed as it had been ever since she arrived home. What if she wasn't in her room? I could feel the terror up in my throat as I carefully opened her door and looked inside. Cass lay asleep on her bed. It was too dark to see her face or her green yellow hair spread out on her pillow.

She was still asleep when I left for work, but Mom called me during the morning. "Cass left a little while ago," she said. "She's going back to Cambridge. Have you spoken to Gary yet?"

"No. He hasn't called me, and I've been afraid to call him."

"It's all right," Mom said. "I told you it would be all right. She's still pretty angry—at all of us—but she'll get over it. I just wanted you to know, because I was sure you were worrying."

Gary met me after work, and we sat down right in the middle of Stonestown Mall, while he told me what had happened.

"I said no," he said, sounding dazed. "I would have called you this morning before you left for work, but we were up so late last night I overslept."

"How late?"

"Oh—maybe three or four. She wouldn't stop. She

kept trying to get me to change my mind. But I said no." He seemed amazed that he had been able to resist her.

"Did she say anything about me?"

"Yes. She said she thought I would hurt you. That I didn't really love you."

"She told me the same thing. She said you were coming to me on the rebound. She thinks you only love her."

"No," Gary said slowly, almost as if it were a brand-new thought. "I don't love her. Not anymore."

A little boy ran by, chasing a rolling ball. Gary put out his foot to stop the ball, bent down, picked it up and handed it to the child. I could feel the relief beginning to warm my insides, but I needed to know one more thing.

"Did she . . . did she . . ."

He didn't know what I was going to ask. He was watching me, waiting for my question.

"Did she say she would ever . . ." It was so hard to put into words. Gary stayed quiet, watching my face. "Did she say she would ever—come back to you? She always used to, Gary. You remember. Did she say . . ."

"No, she didn't."

"But if she did say it, Gary. If you thought she might. Because maybe that's why she doesn't want the two of us to hook up. Maybe she wants to save you for herself. Maybe she's not through with you. Maybe she needs to know you'll always be there waiting for her. Maybe she always thought you would wait, and maybe one day she really would come back to you."

"No." Gary shook his head. "She didn't say anything like that."

He wasn't telling me what I wanted to hear. He didn't even understand what I needed to hear.

"I don't think she wants either of us to get away from her," I said angrily. "She wants to keep us both—but separately. She wants us always to be there when she whistles. I don't think she can stand the two of us having a life together without her."

"No," Gary said. "You're too hard on her. It's not like you, Penny."

"You're a sucker," I said bitterly. "When it comes to her, you'll always be a sucker."

Gary put his hands on either side of my face and held it so that I had to look at him.

"We can both afford to be generous, Penny," he said. "Cass is no wicked witch who can cast a spell over you or me. She's just Cass."

"But if," I said, "if she told you she would come back to you? If you knew it would happen?"

He was grinning at me now.

"Stop it, Gary. Let me finish. If she told you she would, if she . . ."

"If she told me she would," Gary said, very distinctly, "I would tell her no. I would tell her I love Baby Sister."

"Don't call me that, ever again," I snapped.

"I would tell her I love Penny, my lucky Penny, my beautiful Penny, the best in the whole world."

I put my arms around his neck and kissed him again and again right there in the middle of Stonestown Mall. And if Cass had been there, I would have kissed her too.

16

Gary gave me a diamond engagement ring at Christmas.

"I wish it could have been bigger," he said, "but I know we have to save most of our money now."

"It's beautiful, Gary," I told him, holding out my hand and watching the lovely little diamond sparkling on my finger. The ring hadn't come as a surprise. I had given myself a manicure the night before, polishing my fingernails with a deep rose-blush color in preparation.

I gave Gary a wristwatch for Christmas, and I made him a double-breasted gray flannel blazer. For the two of us, I made matching raw silk kimonos in white. "For our trousseau," I told him. "For May."

The marriage date was now set—May twenty-fifth, the day before my birthday, at St. Paul's Church, with a reception afterward at the Francisco Club. My parents had given up trying to persuade me to wait, and Gary's parents, relieved that he wasn't marrying Cass, had approved right from the start.

I had drawn up a Bridal Planning Checklist, and over the next few days, Gary and I needed to sit down and make some decisions. We still weren't sure where we would go on our honeymoon. He preferred Hawaii, but I liked the idea of New York. We could stay at a hotel in the city, and while I was there I could visit some of the famous bridal shops I'd heard about. Maybe part of the trip could be tax-deductible.

We had other things to decide as well—the guest list, announcements, invitations, flowers, the color scheme. . . . Gary wasn't sure if he wanted to wear a white tux or a cream-colored one. But there was no question in my mind about my wedding gown. It was a stunning traditional pattern, with an Alençon lace bodice trimmed with pearls, modified leg-of-mutton sleeves and a soft, satin skirt with chapel train. I had even selected a pattern for my wreath—a pearl and lace design with a fingertip-length veil. My fingers were itching to begin.

Gary's parents invited me and my parents over for Christmas dinner. The food was delicious, and even Darryl seemed in high spirits. Everybody teased me about the way I kept waving my hand around. Mom told Mrs. Summers about her wedding, and Mrs. Summers told Mom about hers. Mom said that her mother had wanted her to have a traditional wedding, but that she had worn a short dress and a hat that was too big. Mrs. Summers said she had worn her own mother's gown, even though the taffeta had been a little stained and some of the seams had split. She looked at me and said, hesitating, "Actually, Penny, if you wanted to wear it, you certainly could. It would need some work, and you'd have to take it in. But since I only have sons, I'm not saving it for anybody else."

"No, no, Mother Summers." (That's what I had started calling her.) "I'm going to make my own dress, but thanks anyway."

"She's going to make mine too," Mom burst in. "I hope she'll let me wear a deep rose color. I look very good in a deep rose."

"I like lavender," Mrs. Summers said.

"Well, I'll make your dress too," I told her.

"Oh, no, Penny," Gary's mother said. "I wouldn't think of it. You'll have enough to do making your own and your mother's."

"I might even go for a dress in a salmon color," Mom said dreamily. "But, of course, Penny has to decide."

"It won't be any trouble, Mother Summers," I said. "I'd be happy to make your dress."

Nobody asked me who was going to be my maid of honor. I had written to Cass in London, asking her, but she hadn't answered. So far she hadn't written at all. So far, she had sent only two picture postcards to my parents, showing a bridge and a clock. I knew Cass would never consent to be my maid of honor, and I was pretty sure she would not come home for the wedding either. But in my mind, I liked to think of her as my maid of honor. I liked to think of her in a pale pink dress with soft petal sleeves, carrying a bouquet of roses as she walked down the aisle. Of course, I would make her the dress. It would fit her perfectly, showing the lines of her full, lovely figure. On her head, I would put a slim coronet of pale flowers and green leaves.

Nobody mentioned Cass. Even at home, my parents did not speak about her—in front of me. After I married, Mom said, she and Dad might sell the house and take a small apartment. All of us knew that Cass would not be coming home again for a long time.

The day after Christmas, I woke up early and hurried into Cass's room. Something had been missing for quite a while, and I couldn't remember what it was. But I had awoken that morning knowing that something was gone. I sat down on Cass's bed and looked around the empty, tidied room. It was hard to believe that Cass had ever lived here.

Now I realized what it was that was missing—the picture of Cass and Gary at the junior prom. Mom must have put it away, and I had never really focused on its disappearance until this morning. I began looking for it—inside Cass's desk, in her closet, her chest. I couldn't find it anywhere.

I sat down again on Cass's bed, and I thought about the way she had looked when she returned home the last time—the way her face was red and swollen from crying, and how she pleaded with me not to marry Gary. I thought about how I wanted to see her at my wedding, walking down the aisle in a lovely pale pink dress that I had made for her, with pink flowers in her hair. And I thought about the picture postcards from England, with the bridge and the clock, that contained no message for me.

Then I got up, went out of Cass's room and began working on my wedding gown.